To Mary,

Best wishes and enjoy The Floodgates.

Daniel L. Wagner
9/27/2014

THE FLOODGATES
Daniel Wagner

AuthorHouse™
1663 Liberty Drive
Bloomington, IN 47403
www.authorhouse.com
Phone: 1-800-839-8640

© 2013 Daniel Wagner. All rights reserved.

No part of this book may be reproduced, stored in a retrieval system, or transmitted by any means without the written permission of the author.

Published by AuthorHouse 5/30/2013

ISBN: 978-1-4817-5284-8 (sc)
ISBN: 978-1-4817-5282-4 (hc)
ISBN: 978-1-4817-5283-1 (e)

Library of Congress Control Number: 2013908721

The picture on the cover is of the author and his mother.

Any people depicted in stock imagery provided by Thinkstock are models, and such images are being used for illustrative purposes only.
Certain stock imagery © Thinkstock.

This book is printed on acid-free paper.

Because of the dynamic nature of the Internet, any web addresses or links contained in this book may have changed since publication and may no longer be valid. The views expressed in this work are solely those of the author and do not necessarily reflect the views of the publisher, and the publisher hereby disclaims any responsibility for them.

For my dearest,
Bonnie,
who has held on tight for the ride.

And for my children,
Zanaya and Zachary,
you're the best.

"The Earth does not belong to us;
we belong to it."
—*Chief Seattle, 1854*

IN EASTERN WASHINGTON SKIES, A hawk soars effortlessly. He searches terrain below for carrion only his sharp eyes will reveal. At his vantage point he can see much of what is called the Great Basin, an area that includes the great coulees and remains of prehistoric ice flows that ravaged the Eastern Washington landscape, giving rise to the architecture that would become the Columbia River and its geographical fingers. Below is the Grand Coulee Dam.

The heavenly predator does not follow the actions of two men on top of the dam's spillways. They look over the 550 feet to the bottom. One of them pitches his beer can over the side and watches as the can arcs effortlessly, tumbling over and over. Briefly, it hangs in midair. Then, as if its course were predestined, it finds the first sprays of water falling over the dam and is swallowed up, leaving nothing to record its history. The two men stand in awe, mouths agape, staring quietly at the power of the cascading water below them. They briefly scan the currents below in a juvenile effort to put closure to their recklessness and littering. Several minutes later, without the finality of a bobbing beer can in a distant current of the river below, they give up and acquiesce to the dam, recognizing their own Lilliputian statures in the face of this leviathan. They turn from the railing and walk away.

Foreword

IN THE BEGINNING, THE DAMMING of the Columbia was the dream of one man, a lawyer by the name of William M. Clapp who lived in Ephrata. Those who lived in the basin agreed with him; they wanted to benefit from the Columbia's resources, to irrigate barren land from which farmers, assorted Indian tribes, and homesteaders had attempted to eke out an existence. Those who lived east of the Cascades learned to live with unforgiving terrain that was infertile, alkaline, and dotted with sagebrush. The harsh, austere land proved to be a spoiler to those who attempted to tame her. Over a period of several years a contentious war ensued: battle lines were drawn, and politics found its way to the choked lands of Eastern Washington.

In the East, the Depression had taken its toll. Long lines of hungry Americans waited patiently for the meager handouts provided in the soup lines. Hoovervilles epitomized the lost dreams of a great industrialized nation that had succumbed to avarice and the greed of speculation, which had gone awry with the 1929 stock market crash. Men, women, and children who once had promise in their hearts now saw nothing but despair. It was from these ranks that a great dam would be built. A new president with an eye for healing the wounds of the nation started the CCC, and the New Deal was born.

In the 1930s, the Columbia flowed from the Canadian border down to the Pacific Ocean. It traced its serpentine length through the eastern portion of Washington State and then ever so gently bent its arm and ran the full breadth of the Washington and Oregon borders. Near Pasco, it met up with the Snake River. They joined, became one, pursued their travels together west, and finally emptied into the sea. The Columbia made its trip through the Northwest for thousands of years, unhindered by dams. The river flowed freely, without the hand of man to change its course or its depth. It continued its travels past the mesas and small towns without notice until Clapp had his dream. Until then, its only and most important resource had been the Steelhead, Chinook, and Coho salmon that fed the Indian tribes up and down her breadth.

Slowly, men, and later women and children, began to arrive in the Eastern Washington towns: Soap Lake, Ephrata, Coulee City, and so on. Towns began to take on the dynamics of apprehension: a great project was in the works and possibly would affect the residents' lives forever. Towns that were small began to grow with the new immigrants; men from all over the country flocked to these lone outposts seeking employment and a chance to make good wages. Thus, construction began on one of the major civil projects of its time.

The Grand Coulee Dam, standing 550 feet tall and nearly a mile long, is a monolith. She stands smack in the middle of nowhere, a testament to the laborers and engineers who built her. Her dimensions are staggering: once called "the world's most monstrous dam," she is reverential, standing tall in the vast basin of the Pacific Northwest.

Construction commenced in the mid-1930s. The undertaking was vast and required no fewer than seven construction companies, with Henry Kaiser at the project's helm. The finer details were worked out by Kaiser himself, the bid was placed, and men and machine began their conquest of the Columbia River.

1. Jake's Story

IN THE VAST COLUMBIA BASIN, farming began to spring up on formerly hardpan, sunbaked soil. The farms were scattered all over the topography of Eastern Washington, from towns as far west as Ellensburg to Spokane on the eastern side of the state. The 1940s brought in young families searching for land and a new life on the high plateaus that overlooked the Columbia River; Jake Ferguson's family was no exception. As men returned home from war, new farms began to spring up. Some were minute, with as little as a couple hundred acres. Others were behemoths encompassing large parts of counties. with acres and acres of planted land. This was part and parcel of the promise provided to the Ferguson family as they took up their plot on the Royal Slope. The Ferguson family's history with the basin began after the declining years of World War II. Jake's father had spent his enlistment in the Pacific theater. On his separation, he decided to take his family to the Pacific Northwest. The family started farming on the Royal Slope overlooking the Columbia River. The farm's assorted crops ranged from corn to hay, with a small hog farm for variety. As Jake grew up, he learned the intricacies of surviving on the plateau overlooking the river. He loved the farm and grew to appreciate the benefits accorded the family from the Columbia's damming.

In the early morning, sunrise would provide early warmth up and down the valleys that run along the Columbia's course. Light would bathe the rocky cliffs overlooking the river, and slowly the canyons and chaparral would take on life as they awakened from their sleep. Jake often drove down to the river from Royal City. He would watch the coming dawn as it traced its finger from the east toward him, spreading pinks, reds, ochres, and every possible color on the palette. After his sanctuary he would slowly walk back to the old Ford F250, climb into the cab, and make the drive back up the hill to Royal City.

Jake's mornings often began on this note; he sought humility in the solace of the great river. He returned to the family farm after a tour in Vietnam with the Marine Corps. Life had never meant so much than on his return back home. He did his best to leave the war behind him, although his memories of firefights and death often crowded his dreams at night. Jake managed to find peace at home. His father was gaining in years, and the farm work was proving to be too much for him. He looked to his sons to take over the burden the farm was becoming, so Jake and his younger brother, Keith, became the inheritors of the land. They were always up before first light and never finished before nightfall, and they fulfilled their father's dream of keeping the farm productive. Jake and Keith had little trouble making their partnership work; each designated to himself the chores he was best at, whether it was mending fence, repairing the farm machinery, or inoculating the livestock. After all, they were a team.

Often, they went into Royal in the morning to grab a bite in the town café, where they ran into their neighbors. If not for the centrally located café and tavern, they probably would have gone weeks without seeing any familiar faces. The locals often would spend an hour or two, depending on time constraints, shooting the bull while digesting their bacon and eggs and keeping the one or two waitresses busy filling their coffee mugs. Life moved slowly in the basin; there was no pretentiousness, simplicity was the order of the day, and Royal City was slow and easy.

Fall, winter, and now spring of 1999 had been foul. The brothers had found themselves in town a little more often than usual. The café in Royal City was often more busy than not, as the weather fronts that passed through the area from the west brought more rain than usual. It was turning out to be one of the wettest years on record, always with the promise of one more inch coming over the Cascades from the fronts that passed over the Pacific. Always the winter meant downtime for the farmers and cattlemen who made their living in the Basin, but now they mulled over weather reports and speculated what would be in store when the spring would finally arrive. On one particularly nasty day, Jake and Keith found themselves inundated with the rains. They hurried about the farm securing equipment and tying down loose ends, as the wind had taken a notion to blow, making this particular day a little more interesting than the norm. They cussed each other above the howling wind and fought off the rain as their tempers flared. Finally, the whole exercise became one of futility, and the storm won the round. They finally gave up and drove off to town for a hot cup of coffee and a little bit of gossip.

    They sat down at a booth. Already they could see that the rain and wind had brought many of their neighbors in to share in their discord. Many were grumbling about the mud and equipment that had become bogged down. The rains were unforgiving; even the Columbia was looking wider and a little dangerous. Most of the old cowpokes and farmers stayed at the café longer than their usual two cups of coffee and scoffed at going back to their spreads and tackling the weather again. As morning ticked away, newspapers were discarded. At one end of the counter, a *Spokesman Review* lay in a heap, crumpled with the exception of part of one article: "YORK—the Nuclear Regulatory Commission has suspended any Y2K testing at the Peach Bottom nuclear plant after the facility's monitoring computers crashed for seven hours during testing last month." The article finished by adding that technicians were testing new software that monitored one of the plant reactors. The plant was almost three thousand miles away, and on a shitty day in early March it was not of much interest to these locals ruminating over their quandary with nature.

The rains that lasted through the end of '98 and well into the beginning of '99 brought much concern and speculation to the hydrologists and reclamation experts, who watched as the Pacific Northwest took beating after beating of torrential rains. The water had no place to run off and clogged storm drains in low-lying areas, rapidly filling them to excess until cities and towns alike found themselves with streets flooded. Mudslides prevailed wherever the rains had fallen. The calamities continued well into March, when a somewhat ominous tone had taken hold in a region already known for its above normal precipitation.

The Columbia, too, had become more vigorous, its strength embellished by the weather fronts that had provided the rains. The dams that held back its confluence now had waters lapping high upon their spillways, pushing hard at the barriers that kept back the river's flow. Reclamation districts intent on irrigating a once-arid land were now faced with a new dilemma, flooding. Sound decisions and reasoning gave way to abstraction as policymakers tried to figure their way through a multitude of problems that seemed to rise faster than the water level of the Columbia.

The Henderson farm was fast becoming an exception to the patterns of family farms in America, most of which were lingering bastions of debt. Often the families were delinquent in the bank payments owed the land and machinery they used to cultivate and harvest their crops. Speculation on fall crops often led to failure; banks would foreclose on a minute's notice, and a family's home for generations would fall to the auctioneer's gavel. Jake and Keith witnessed this often around Royal City. They went to the auctions themselves, sometimes in hopes of picking up used machinery at bargain prices but more often than not out of curiosity about who had lost the latest round to the bank.

This year was proving to be more difficult for the farming and cattle ranchers in the basin. Many had hoped for a little less of the rain that had wreaked havoc on their land and livestock. Jake himself became more cynical about the future; they also were under a mountain of debt, with unpaid bills for seed, machinery, and other miscellaneous items needed to keep the farm running. Often, they were overwhelmed and could have used an extra man to keep things running smoothly. Downtime on machinery was difficult to absorb, and when parts were needed for repair, it was often cash that had to be used and not credit. Finally, on a Friday morning in late January, Casper Henderson had his first stroke.

Jake and Keith were always up before 5:00 a.m. They began the morning ritual by milling around in the kitchen, stretching, scratching, and often going outside to catch a glimpse of daybreak or take a smoke. There were no women in the household. Their mother had died long ago, a statistic to cancer, and both sons had failed marriages. As they got the coffee ready, the old hound began scratching laboriously at Casper's door.

Their father was always up long before the household stirred, often frying up bacon and eggs, but today silence greeted Jake when he came into the kitchen. Nothing was suspect until the dog's scratching became more desperate. They entered the room and found Casper on the floor, one side moving and the other paralyzed. No sound issued from his lips, just drooling and heavy breathing as he tried to mouth words. Jake noticed that the left side of his face seemed to be frozen in a drooping position. The brothers hurriedly picked him up and carried him through the house to Casper's car in the front yard. All their movements were deliberate and methodical as they positioned the old man in the backseat as comfortably as possible for the long drive to the nearest hospital, some thirty miles away.

The morning moved at a fast pace. After they found Casper on the floor, minutes became hours. They didn't have the option of making a 911 call; they were too far off to have the intervention of an emergency team to be effective. Time was of the essence, and they parlayed what little they had into immediate action. They drove as quickly as possible to Moses Lake with Keith keeping a watchful eye on their father and Jake doing the driving. They got there in record time. Casper had survived the stroke up until this point, and they were able to get him in the hospital in the ICU. The brothers stayed in the hospital waiting room for the rest of the day while the doctors did a battery of tests to determine the extent of the stroke and look for other clots that could move and threaten his life. By six o'clock, they had been at the hospital all day. They checked in on Casper to find he was sleeping and returned home.

They returned using I-90, and as they finally came in view of the Columbia below, Jake told Keith that the river looked higher than normal. His eyes had grown accustomed to seeing the river at all angles and depths. Keith shrugged off his comment but took a sidelong glance and agreed. Then he decided that it was the way the moon was hitting the surface, casting an illusion of sorts. They got home at about eight. The house and outbuildings were eerily silent at first, but when they got out of the car the dog came around the house barking and curling up his lip as if to say hello. The pigs started grunting loudly in anticipation of finally getting fed.

2. CHRIS

AT FIFTEEN, CHRIS WAS TALL and slender, with striking features that appealed to the attentions of girls in his class. He would have preferred that they not notice him, but that proved to be folly. He was often absorbed and moved in a small circle of close friends who had similar interests and aptitudes. They were considered the nerds of the high school, as it is customary for adolescents to label the extraordinary kids who didn't fit in or moved in different directions. Chris's group consisted of six boys, all of approximately the same age and intellectual capacity. They were the brightest of the bright, and their worlds consisted of their preoccupation with lofty goals and quantum mechanics as well as the computer keyboard. Chris early on had exposure to the realm of cyberspace; he found it fascinating and became mesmerized by all the information he could gain with no more than a few typed commands. He would often spend hours at the keyboard on weekends. Instead of going out to the nearest mall with friends, he would be surfing the net.

Chris's preoccupation with computers was in part the doings of his parents. Both had been transplanted to the Seattle area in the late eighties, and both were in lockstep with many other young and middle-aged professionals who fell into the technological fields. They felt at home in the Pacific Northwest among big companies such as Microsoft. They moved from the smog and overcrowding of the LA area to live quietly in the Queen Anne neighborhood of northwest Seattle. Their view afforded them a sweeping panorama of the Puget Sound and the Space Needle. They could watch the ferries as they floated back and forth between Bremerton and the San Juans. In reality, they were living the dream of many others who had pursued this vision but were unable to obtain it.

Chris grew up pampered as the only child of Dave and Celia. Like other children of the new age professionals of Seattle, he often got what he wanted, when he wanted it, and discarded it after the novelty had worn off. He was a spoiled child and at times difficult. As Chris reached adolescence, his interest in technology began to become insatiable. His father purchased a computer and printer for Chris's room. At that point his world took a sudden change that would forever impact his life.

3. BPA

THE COLOSSUS THAT WOULD RUN the great works of the Northwest, oversee its dams and its river navigation, and run the power grid that provided electricity to four western states and beyond was the BPA, the Bonneville Power Administration. Its influence was felt throughout the West, as it dictated the policies and outcomes of millions of lives and businesses. The BPA has long been the envy of its East Coast neighbors, who for years had fallen prey to the greed of corrupt politicians and other savvy opportunists. The BPA had its fingertips on the natural resources of the Columbia River and its tributaries. It was with this great river that would eventually empty into the Pacific that the administration could feed the hungry consumers who longed for electricity to light their cities with a cheap source of energy from its harnessed currents. From its headquarters in Portland, Oregon, the BPA would delegate its authority, make policy, and implement change that affected the lives of so many.

Dave sat quietly at his desk in the waning hours of daylight; he stared resolutely at the screen in front of him as night started to cast its first pall over Portland. The city outside his window was starting to bristle with nightlife, honking horns, and pedestrians hurriedly making their ways to dinner dates and bistros for entertainment or a round of drinks with colleagues at the corner bar. Dave was working late and had been for several months. After his separation from his wife, he found no reason to go to an empty apartment that offered only drab walls and not the squealing and playing of his two small children. The custody of his children was already predetermined: Dave decided that a legal battle would be too costly and settled for visitation. He quietly got up and walked over to the hallway as if to search for life. At this time of the day, the BPA administration building was a study in shadows, dim except for a few offices.

He returned to his screen and keyboard to make further inquiries about the Columbia's currents and depths. He was extremely thorough, as he was troubled by the amounts of rain and snowfall that could impact the region's capabilities to handle the excess when the spring warmth returned. The Cascades had record snowfalls, along with the several hard rains that had pelted the Northwest. He eagerly searched through data to gauge what the near future would bring. As an engineer, Dave was well versed on the hydrology of the river. He knew that there was more-than-adequate flow through the numerous dam generators to keep the area lit, but in the recesses of his mind a more ominous question was being formed. He typed in more information and patiently waited for the responses to materialize. The answers confirmed some of his worries. Most of what he asked was hypothetical in regards to El Niño, but in combination with the Y2K question, he decided further research was needed.

4. Billy Red Bones

Billy was the last of his people, the Wanapum. His tribe, like many other Indian tribes, had once populated the length of the Columbia. They were proud and independent. Billy drew strength from his people's bloodlines, but now he was alone. Billy often found himself staring up at the high cliffs and plateaus that looked down on the river. He rejoiced in the Columbia's strength and would daydream of days spent on its shores, spearfishing the spawning salmon as they fought their way up the current. That was all gone now—the makeshift platforms where young men would aim their spears into the currents and whole families would gather at the river's edge to celebrate a day's catch—all those beautiful days gone, victim to the progress of the newcomers who had dammed the river and slowed the progress of the mighty salmon forever. Billy still lived near the river; his home was simple, for he was a man of modest means. But he also was a dignitary of sorts, a shaman—or medicine man, if you prefer. Tucked away off the road, his home sat quietly in a remote area surrounded by a few trees and sagebrush. An old Shasta trailer with a plywood-and-tarpaper addition for extra room was Billy's castle. He shared this desert home with a few rattlesnakes. They often would slither from one corner to the other and would extend greetings to old friends of Billy's, especially on hot days. His serpentine friends were often used in religious rituals.

Billy still walked the river edge. He watched the silent currents and judged its mysteries often while looking for relics of ancient ancestors who had hunted the Columbia before him. He lived in Beverly, which was nothing more than an exit off the highway to the bigger cities of Richland and Pasco. Across the river was Vantage and nothing more except Schawana, a lone gas station, and the tumbleweed that always seemed to be in the road. He had been spending more time at the river, and he had noticed that landmark rocks were disappearing under the water's surface. Gradually, as the months had drawn closer to spring and the climate had warmed, the water level had risen significantly. He felt that in the near future the spillways on Wanapum would be opened to capture the excess and generate power, and the river would again return to its old levels. That did not happen.

High in the Cascades, the winter snows started piling up in early October and kept adding inch upon inch until several feet were beneath the men sent out to measure the levels. The heavy metal measuring sticks often sank entirely beneath the snow. They men shook their heads, alarmed by the amounts of snowfall that had fallen. There were concerns of avalanches, but more significant was the danger of flood following a fast melt.

The men and women who worked in the government offices, the reclamation districts, and other signature arms of bureaucracy began to analyze data that were updated daily. Rivers and lakes were beginning to rise, and contingency plans had to be put into effect.

Billy took one of his meandering walks down to the river in late March. He looked beyond the river toward Vantage and thought hard about how things had once been, long before the repeated damming, when life was quieter. The multitudes who eventually began to move into the area were ignorant of the history of the river; they built large, expensive homes with sweeping views and vistas that overlooked the Columbia. They were a decadent society seeking instant gratification with their wealth. Billy looked at these interlopers, who now encroached on the once-sacred land of the Wanapum, with disgust. He felt that they were trespassers who would ruin this land with their new communities and their wineries spreading randomly up and down the river's length. If only one of nature's disasters could bring these new pioneers to their knees. Billy thought of May 18, 1980, a beautiful Sunday morning when a mountain claimed much of the land he loved with its ash. *We need another Mt. St. Helens.* With that, he picked up a small disc of a rock and skipped it across the water's surface.

5. Casper's Stroke

Casper returned home from his hospital stay on a Saturday afternoon. His left side had improved, but it was still flaccid and without the old strength that had carried him through many years of hard work. His speech now was almost inaudible, part of the telltale signs of aphasia, the lingering mark of being a stroke survivor. His eyes, dull gray with a hint of vexation, were now the only means of expression for the man who was once the patriarch of his family. Casper was not an ideal patient; his stubborn, obstinate nature proved a challenge to the doctors, nurses, and therapists who had been responsible for his care. He would often struggle with them, his conscious mind disorganized and delusional from the life-threatening blood clot that was starving his brain for oxygen. He survived nonetheless. Casper gradually became stronger; his will had kept him alive. During his hospital stay he was able to improve, and although not entirely independent, he was capable of getting his needs met.

Into the second week of his hospital stay, Jake and Keith began to see an improvement in the old man's resolve. His anger and frustration were starting to come back, and although his speech was a word salad, his cussing was accurate, especially when he wanted to make a point. Casper would spend a total of another three weeks in his convalescence before finally gaining the privilege of returning home to the farm and a more sedentary existence. In the meantime he had the daily nagging of the nurses and therapists, who pushed him through the grind of physical therapy and relearning old skills that had once been so easy for him.

Caspar came home from Moses Lake down I-90 on a warm April day. The station wagon's windows were rolled down. Casper sat in the backseat, gradually attempting to reposition himself as they got closer to the river as if to get a better view. The rising lava rocks stood majestically over the water below. Casper felt invigorated as the scenery unfurled before him, the sky a brilliant blue. The distant screech of meadowlarks filled and greeted him on his return home.

As the boys began to round the last corner before the ride up the hill to Royal City, Casper looked one more time at the Columbia. He thought it looked higher than he had remembered. He then shook his head, feeling that the stroke had robbed him of his vision.

6. The Hacker

CHRIS WAS FINDING THE COMPUTER to be a tool of his liking, the keyboard a perfect extension of the id, the ego, and an adolescent's flight into uncharted territories. At any hour of the day he could enter into a world that would reveal secrets that others only dreamed of. Chris was fast becoming an adroit hacker, and there was no stopping him in his new enterprise. He would launch himself into new dimensions while he sat in front of his screen and keyboard and nobody, not even his parents, was the wiser. He developed a keen interest in breaking the everyday codes that were supposed to prohibit entry into the secret worlds of technology. Chris found many of the codes an easy target. He broke into their systems easily, often leaving a calling card or virus to be remembered by. In his ambitions he did not visualize himself as a criminal; he felt that his achievements were innocent and could not fathom the concerns of those who discovered his calling cards of cyberspace disruption. The dexterous movements of fingers on the keyboard were proving to be addictive, and as he specialized and perfected his art he became more emboldened. He was careful not to leave incriminating evidence of his wanderings, and he was surgical in his delivery and diverse. He even managed to gain information from a local software company and get away clean. He was gradually becoming interested in bigger targets.

The preoccupation for bigger and better targets kept him busy through the night. While his parents slept, Chris would log in and search the computer screen for opportunities to invade other systems. These targets of opportunity were many and diversified, ranging from the mundane to area department stores. He was finding that this access was giving him a feeling of power, almost invincibility, as he created havoc in various computer banks and systems. In the beginning he felt that this was just an innocent way of having some adolescent fun. He could not recognize the birth of his addiction. He slowly increased the amounts of time spent in his curiosity until the infancy of his journey on the screen was reaching maturity.

Chris committed his first act of fraud on a February night. A friend who had been failing in a chemistry class was worried about his grade point average. He knew Chris spent time on the computer and decided to ask him if he could gain some information on his grades. After dinner and his exit from the table that evening, Chris sat down at his computer and slowly and painstakingly began his search for the secrets his friend had requested. After hours of trying various accesses and codes, he was able to break into the school's system and recover the chemistry grades. His friend's worries were well founded.

Chris became bored with these picayune targets and found new avenues of experimentation, which included wiping off the monthly credit card charges of friends who could not contain their shopping spree charges at area malls. Chris now sought bigger prizes, something with risk that could get the adrenaline pumping. He eventually keyed into the BPA's computers.

7. Dave

DAVE HAD HIS CHILDREN OVER the weekend. After taking them back on a Sunday afternoon, he found himself in an antagonistic spirit. Upon dropping them off at their mother's home, he argued with her about the restraints of visitation and support. He felt that the balance was tilted her way and he was being alienated by the courts on every plateau. The conflict got him nowhere; his ex was as stubborn as he was. She viewed custody and support as nonissues, and besides, she was asserting her independence and following in the rank and file of the career woman. Dave gave the kids final good-bye hugs and kisses, traded some friendly punches, and told them to make plans for the next time he would be seeing them.

He left their home feeling mad and empty, but this Sunday was a bright and sunny one, a unique occurrence for the Portland area when so many days were dark, dismal, and rainy. After a moment's hesitation, he aimed the car up I-5, drove until the Route 84 exit, and found himself going east up the Columbia Gorge. He looked at the beauty of the gorge and the width of the river. He could see the tiny vehicles on the Washington side. He passed Hood River. The wind surfers who were always plentiful during the warmer months were not to be seen; it was still a little brisk even for them. Dave drove up to Goldendale in Washington and then returned along the Washington side, stopping only to have a burger at White Salmon, a small town with a unique view of the Columbia. Below he could see the Hood River, one or two barges heading up or down the river, and the traffic on the other side. The elevation gave White Salmon an extremely good vantage point of the river's energy and commerce. He looked down at the river with the trained eye of his profession. Dave knew the river and could see that it had widened. He decided he would have to tackle this issue in the near future.

The following day when Dave sat down to work, the office was still vacant. He came in earlier than his coworkers, hoping to find answers more easily with fewer distractions. As he waited for the computer to warm up, staring blankly at the screen and thought back to the previous day's trip. Finally he was in the system pecking out his questions of depths, currents, flows and reservoir capacities. Then he noticed the glitch. At first it did not register to Dave that a virus could be in the system; the BPA had gone to great lengths to secure all their systems with the technology of the day. They had enough firewalls in place to deter any hacker, but the anomaly was there all the same.

Dave made a mental note that security would have to be notified immediately and precautions would have to be taken.

8. Kettle Falls

At the beginning of the Columbia's journey into the interior of Washington lay Kettle Falls, far beyond the Henderson farm and Billy Red Bones. Kettle Falls rested at the foot of Lake Roosevelt, where tourists come in the spring and summer to spend time with the family, recreate, and relax in the cabins along the lake.

The visitors particularly fell in love with the lake, the 150 miles of water backed up by Grand Coulee Dam, a volume of water so great that in a small way was said to offset the magnetic poles of the earth. The Blue Moons owner—or, to the locals, Ned—was flush with facts. He could give all the specifics of the area, detail the monumental task of building the dam, and describe the lake and its population, no more than a couple thousand indigenous folks and neighbors to the Colville Indian Reservation to the west. Lake Roosevelt was essential to the local tourist industry in the way of sightseeing, fishing, boating, camping and the other usual summertime activities. At the Blue Moon hunting lodge, the proprietor watched the comings and goings of these seasonal adventurers with curiosity and cynicism. Year after year these big-city travelers found their way up to his lodge to do some recreating. Ned would continue on with these evening conversations as long as he had an audience remaining, often to the boredom of his guests.

In the early spring he became aware of the heavy snowpack that coated the Cascades. He knew that the lake would be deep and was beginning to see the signs of heavy runoff along the shore. The waves lapped higher along the coastline than in previous years. His cabins sat far enough away from the lake for safety, but he still felt a twinge of alarm as he saw the early spring thaw.

Generally he would equate the deep blue of the lake and its extra depth with the better economics it would provide. The deeper waters invited more tourists, campers, fishermen, and those who wanted to enjoy the scenery, but he viewed the lake's charm with trepidation and felt that there was something ominous in the cool waters from which he had derived his living.

Ned began to take daily trips down to the lake and along the rocky shoreline. As March became April and then May, he began to see the subtle changes of the Cascade melting. Water was gradually inching up around the shoreline, and the lake was much deeper than in previous years. He had never taken any interest in the depth of the lake before, but along with the snow they had also had more rain than usual, which finally led to his current curiosity and his daily habit of watching the lake. Ned chose not to alarm anyone with his findings; he attributed a lot of his concerns to the fact that he was getting older, more paranoid, and out of touch. He kept a low profile to avoid arousing the suspicions of his neighbors that he was getting a little senile. As the families, hostels, and bed and breakfasts that surrounded the lake began to wake from their winter's sleep, they too began to notice that the lake was becoming more foreboding.

9. Nora

SULLEN AND STILL BEAUTIFUL AT thirty-eight, Nora was unable to find her way out of Royal City. A trail of relationships gone awry and a failed marriage left her almost penniless and cynical about the world she lived in. Her children no longer lived with her, preferring to stay with their father in Spokane, so she lived quietly in town in an apartment inhabited by herself and a stray cat she had found years ago when it came meowing to her door. Her life was uncomplicated at this point. Her rent was cheap, as she worked in her uncle's café and lived in the building that housed it, part of her uncle's great empire. He was fair enough; often he did not charge her rent, but also he would forget to pay her, so she was frugal with the tips she earned in the hash joint downstairs.

The farmers, truck drivers, and assorted others who frequented the Royal Café enjoyed her quick and sharp wit. She pulled no punches when the occasional hay jockey or truck driver would try to pull one over on her: she would cut through their bull and let fly with an assortment of biting remarks and cursing, only to soften up her stance and let them get by with a soft and feminine reminder of who they were talking too. She had left the security of Royal City more than once, always looking for a better life. But she had always returned, a little more cynical, a little more used up, and a little wiser. She was not well traveled, and her destinations when she had left the confines of Royal City had always been a mystery to those closest to her. She lived in Seattle and then would come back and head for Billings, Montana. She was no stranger to Greyhound and all the little towns along the way.

Time passed easily in Royal. With Nora's last return home, she had decided that the highway was no home. She wanted to forget the past, the loss of her kids to her ex-husband, the hard ways of moving around, and the sleepless, unloving nights with strangers she met at corner bars. After her last exodus from Royal, she returned on a winter's day in 1997 with nothing but the clothes on her back and a worn-out Samsonite suitcase.

She found it easy to return, fill in a vacancy at her uncle's café, and reinvent herself. The patrons all knew her and had followed the chaos of her life as she had grown to be a young woman. They had seen her soured relationships and marriage, her flights from town, and her returns. They also knew that age had a way of slowing one's preoccupation with wanderlust, and they figured that she was back to stay.

On her return back to Royal City, she was still fighting the anger from her last soured relationship, with a professional something-or-other who to this day escaped defining. She was always getting tied down with men who had promised her everything but the moon, but after a few months the novelty of connection and lust grew thin as veneer. She never blamed her paramours for the loss but knew it was a combination of facts that often led to her either leaving a relationship or being left.

She eased into life at the café in the spring, at first working part time and then picking up more time as one of the more senior waitresses became involved with a farmer from George and began to miss more and more days of work. Nora found herself a permanent fixture at the restaurant.

As she became more comfortable with the whims of the locals, she started to place names with the faces that often greeted her at the counter and tables. They were a hard group but friendly, and they were quick to admonish one another not to offend the ears of a lady if one cussed a little too loud. She felt at home and was quickly becoming liked for her openness and candor with the boys.

Nora had seen Jake and his brother on occasion; they often came in when the café would first open up in the morning. She often made a mental note of the customers who came in, remembering their preferred times of day, likes, and dislikes, like any good waitress who knew the best way to a tip. She also knew that neither Jake nor Keith said much; they were reserved and quick to find a booth a little removed from the usual commotion and conversation of the other farmers and ranchers that made up the morning chorus of the café. Nora started to notice Jake more often than not. She liked the way he quietly entered the café and put his hat on the table, never too obvious with his demeanor. He was never loud or vulgar and was almost a little shy. She began to put the remnants of her last failed romance into the recesses of her mind and took a more active interest in Jake.

Jake, too, was beginning to notice Nora. She stirred something inside of him, a feeling of warmth that had long been dormant, and now he wanted to know those feelings again. It wasn't long before their intrigue for each other, fueled with a little help from others who dined in the café, encouraged the two to start seeing each other.

10. The Virus

Dave went to work on Friday morning bleary-eyed and shaking off the remnants of a hangover. He and some of his colleagues had decided to go out and have a few at the local sports bar. Dave was looking for an excuse to get out and kick up his heels; he needed some frivolity and hell-raising to get him through the changes he was dealing with. He was now seeing his lawyer on a weekly schedule just to keep up with the demands of his estranged wife. Her needs and wants were rapidly bankrupting him, and the legal fees of $150 an hour placed more stress on him. He welcomed the break from the reality of dealing with an almost-ex-wife and other obligations with wild abandon.

In the office he saw others of his ilk quietly shuffling along as to not be disturbed by some obnoxious noise, looking for silence and the inner sanctums of offices or cubicles. Conversation was spare as the party boys of the previous evening's entertainment sought relief either at the water cooler or the coffeepot.

Dave sat down to his keyboard and screen and signed on. Although his head was still throbbing from the previous night's festivities, he had serious work to do, and the screen in front of him would be a distraction from his current problems. He had been troubled by his recent trip up the Columbia. The rainfall and snowpack would soon be part of a complicated picture, adding not only depth behind the many dams on the Columbia but also a potential for flooding. He watched as characters and figures danced in front of him, showing information on total river flow, irrigation, and power transformation over the large power grid that serviced the four states constituting the Northwest. The replies were automatic and rapid. A whole power structure was now before him as he keyed in more questions and occasionally moved the mouse to highlight specific areas of interest.

Dave was thoroughly enticed with the facts before him; he took little notice at first when a glitch began to develop in his program again. His first response was the same as the previous week, when he thought that a virus had been planted. Security had supposedly checked out the sight, the necessary authorities had been alerted, and a few days later, he had been notified that all was well and good: no virus or hacker was in the system. But yet here was another ambiguity that was unexplained. He felt he could pursue his own leads without jeopardizing the integrity of the entire system. He spent a few quiet moments reflecting on the debacle before him, his mind roaming all the usual suspects, remembering some of the personalities who had gained notoriety for their daring. One in particular he recalled by the name of Kevin Mitnick. Dave dismissed him, however; he was still in jail.

Dave again shut down his system, perplexed by his own lack of knowledge into the underside of the technology that was testing him now. He decided to take a brief break from his morning's work and sit down with a few of his comrades to do some troubleshooting. Maybe the problem was an obvious one, and if not, other avenues would have to be followed aggressively.

The following week Dave and his coworkers applied

themselves diligently to the task of checking and rechecking their systems. They searched through the entire grid system looking for a replicating virus that would be able to wreak havoc on the entire power structure of the Northwest if the problem wasn't solved. Over the period of the following week they searched through their mainframes and tested transmission lines. They reshuffled the power grids, changed the generation capacity of the huge turbines in the dams to see if any problems would arise with the generation of electricity, and even tested the opening and closing of the spillways that controlled the flow of the Columbia. They came up empty handed, and after testing and retesting they came away confident that the system was intact.

11. SYSTEMS

CHRIS HAD FOUND HIS WAY into the computer system of the BPA, and he was becoming a regular visitor to their site. He was exuberant with his cunning, his uncanny ability to break into a system that was thought to be secure. He logged into and out of their system proficiently, and he was able to break their code. He knew that with discovery passwords would be changed and security analysts would set traps, and he was able to circumvent these ploys ingeniously. He eventually came across some traps set for him, small, inconspicuous anomalies in the program that would catch those who tried to hack away at the security of the BPA's systems, but he was too knowledgeable about these insidious techniques and could easily see through their attempts.

Chris was familiar with the risks of his adventures in cyberspace; he was aware of the problems that could arise with his capability of logging into and out of the BPA's system. In spite of a few of the traps that he had encountered, he was enjoying the cat-and-mouse game that he was playing with the security analysts on the other side of the screen. Eventually Chris would leave his calling card, but this came at a later time; for now, he was satisfied with opening and closing the door.

At school the year was winding down. Summer was just around the corner, and Chris and his friends would seek summer employment, talk about college and generally horse around, and go on family trips. Chris felt that with his conquest came bragging rights. He couldn't wait to tell his small group of intellectual friends and fellow computing prodigies, about his capabilities. He knew that being able to get into the BPA would win him high esteem. His was a unique opportunity, and he couldn't wait to tell the others.

His aptitudes, his technique, and the knowledge that he alone stood head and shoulders above the others in being able to break into a system that was supposed to be infallible bolstered Chris. In the early part of April he finally told a few close friends about his recent forays into the BPA power grids. His clique at first felt that he was incapable of such an event, they too had randomly broke into various systems and tested their ingenuity at circumventing the roadblocks to prevent high-tech burglary, but none of them had taken the steps that Chris had taken. They were envious of him, but they all agreed to remain silent on his undertakings.

12. Billy's Jail Stay

Billy returned home after several days in jail in Grant County. As for his ancestors, the drink had caused his judgment to go south. He went into Royal City on a Friday afternoon after a quiet morning and decided that a beer would quench a considerable thirst. After several he had a few minor arguments and at that point decided he should take his business elsewhere. He headed for Moses Lake, taking back roads so as not to arouse the suspicions of the state patrol. Avoiding the interstate, he erratically made his way into town in the late afternoon without apprehension. Billy spent the next several hours in and out of the bars up and down Main Street; he finally wound down after a fight with two comrades whom he had met in his travels led to his arrest for public drunkenness and disorderly conduct. He was booked, fingerprinted, and photographed, all before he was shown his suite for the next several nights.

Billy woke up the next morning feeling the injustices of having too much to drink the day before. His cell was home to six other snoring and flatulent prisoners in various stages of sleep and drunkenness. Billy looked around his surroundings and decided not to put too much effort into getting up. After all, he couldn't recall if he even had enough money to bail out. The day wore on, and finally his roommates began to stir as the beginnings of another day infused the air. Breakfast began, and the routine of coffee and mush begin to wake even the soundest sleepers of this groggy crew.

Billy spent the next several days in jail, after court on the following Monday. He was unable to pay his fine, so he sat it out. The money he had was spent, and his car had been towed away. He was able to reach a friend the following week and borrowed enough money to pay off the remainder of his fine and catch a ride back home.

He talked little to his friend on the ride back home; he was a little humiliated by his behavior. He had had a long dry spell until this recent fall from the wagon, so he chose not to discuss the events of the previous week and look back upon it as history. He knew that the alcohol was bad medicine for him, but he found that once he started there was no satisfying his need. He suffered his mistake in the muted silence and felt that he would not make the same mistake again.

As Billy got out of the car, he thought to himself that he would have to make some other arrangements in order to reclaim the car he had left behind in Moses Lake. For now, he would have to be satisfied with pedestrian travel or friends who could provide him with transportation.

Over the period of the next several days, Billy found himself ruminating about his recent difficulties. His weakness for drink had consumed him, and he felt that he needed to purge himself of temptations. He was again feeling strong and sound; he was beginning to take long walks in the early morning and evening, often down to the river to watch its ebbs and flows. He meditated at the Columbia's shores often and again began to notice that the river was rising in its level. He did not pursue his thoughts about this revelation; he had seen it rise many times before only to return to its normal level. But although he wasn't focusing on what his eyes were revealing to him, he felt a strange and unexplainable gnawing in his gut that would not go away.

13. Casper

Casper remembered very little of the near-death experience he had several weeks ago when his sons had found him on the bedroom floor, the victim of his first stroke. In his convalescence he had regained much of his strength. Although he still had some residual weakness and difficulty speaking at times, he was again capable of letting his sons know what was on his mind. He was still strong physically, and as the Henderson patriarch he was very much involved with the day-to-day activities and assorted other details that were involved with running the farm. He worked with a physical therapist, who came a few days a week and put Casper through a strenuous routine of physical exercises designed to teach his weak side to regain its old energies and restore some of his momentum. Although Casper was often ambivalent about the therapist's visits, he could also see that he was improving gradually. Casper often would let fly with a rash of obscenities when the exercises became too rigorous and monotonous, but he also realized that if he was going to have any degree of normalcy in his life, he would have to complete the intense regimen.

Casper eventually was regaining his old spirit. He again found himself interested in the farm, and now that Jake was seeing Nora, Casper looked forward to the occasional visits from her when she came out to the ranch. The house was now being blessed with the feminine touch, which had not been part of the household since the passing of his wife several years before. Nora would often come unannounced; she was always welcome and still a beautiful, young, and vibrant woman, Casper enjoyed her company and her energy. He often wondered what she saw in Jake, but he was never able to understand how and what women saw in their partners. It was good to have a voice that was higher than theirs at the house.

Casper had been a fixture in the Royal City area for decades, settling in the area after World War II. He brought his young and pregnant wife from Virginia with not an inkling of what he needed to do to run a farm, but he was a gambler and he was young. He used his VA money to buy what land he could and embarked on a dream to become self-sufficient living off the land. He had many tough years, and farming took its toll. Often the only ones to make money were the middleman and the bank, but somehow Casper was able to stay ahead of liens and foreclosures, and that in itself was success.

Casper now sat easily in the overstuffed lazy boy he enjoyed so much. He may have been robbed of some of his physical attributes, but he wasn't denied his strength of spirit, his fortitude, and his longing to stay alive. He had decided in his own being that he would be able to continue to oversee the running of the farm, to always be conspicuous, and to be abreast of all the nuances that one had to be aware of when involved with this type of operation. He declined the opportunity his sons had given him to semiretire; that would be as insidious as death. He had seen other men his age retire only to die soon thereafter. No, that was not the answer now. Casper remained in control, as big a headache as ever. Although Jake and Keith often wished he would pass the baton to them, they knew that in his own way Casper was indispensable.

14. KIRK

THE GEOLOGY DEPARTMENT AT CENTRAL Washington College was inconspicuous, as departments go. It was unobtrusive; funding for it was always a last priority compared to other, more popular departments. However, it had made some impacts. Its professor had been published several times, and there was always the chance of making a rare find that had been overlooked before. The instructor of the department was youthful, full of exuberance and energy; he was out in the field more often than in the classroom. He wanted his students to share in the enthusiasm, the thirst for knowledge, that had taken him over much of the ancient strata of the Northwest and beyond. His contemporaries called him many things; many thought he was eccentric and possibly a little bit crazy. Often aloof and preoccupied by the mysteries of the rocks, to his colleagues he was as enigmatic as the subject matter he taught. To those who were guided by his expertise in geology, he was an icon. Dr. Kirk Johnson was a man destined for great things; his students all were tacitly aware of this.

In the spring, Dr. Johnson had made plans for his fledglings to take part in an outside laboratory. It was the time of the year when many outcroppings now would reveal themselves to the naked eye. The rocks long hidden by winter snow and ice were washed clean with the warming spring thaws. Strata would now give away their long-hidden secrets, and detailed analysis would become imminent. This was what Kirk had envisioned when he took his students over to an area just above the Grand Coulee Dam.

The young doctor had come about his search of the cold and granite cliffs he had explored innocently; he was a young undergrad at the University of Washington, more interested in chemistry and a career in chemical engineering, when a sudden turn of events had altered his course: the eruption of Mount St. Helens. With that his interest in chemistry waned, and he soon became enthralled with his new love. He sought out the experts of the field, often bantering and cajoling them for their founts of knowledge. He had grown amazed by continental shelves, the formation of volcanoes, and the movement of magma. He felt that he could make a major impact in the field and took to his study like a zealot.

Kirk and his entourage left the CWU campus on Thursday afternoon and drove the hundred-plus miles over to the coulee area in a matter of a couple hours. They still had daylight left on the mid-April day, and the weather was nonthreatening and warm. They set up a makeshift camp complete with their tools, picks, shovels, and assorted other instruments so crucial to their discipline. After the task was completed, they headed into one of the nearest towns, where they ate a quick dinner and then went on to a have a few beers at the local watering hole before their return to camp.

The following day was Friday. They awoke early, a little fuzzy from the previous evening's festivities but anxious to get to work. Kirk had chosen a plateau which overlooked Lake Roosevelt and promised a magnificent view of much of the area. One could easily see the past ravages of a land that was formed by glaciers and volcanoes. Kirk looked down on their youthful faces, many of which had first-growth beards. Others were freshly scrubbed, almost adolescent. There was an equal mix of young men and women, all seeking the holy grail of geology. They were his brightest and most promising students; he would have nothing less in his search of terrain. As the students listened intently to their professor's plans for the day, they saw the morning receive its first eastern light. The sun gradually bathed the old faces of the volcanic rock and cast its fingers over Lake Roosevelt, its waters twinkling, almost laughing at the sun. The day promised to be a fruitful one, and the warming of the earth seemed an omen of things to come.

Kirk's students took to their task with enthusiasm. They had waited throughout the winter months to go out into the field and pursue their knowledge in the natural laboratory of the Columbia Basin's geographical reaches. The students were well prepped; they had a brilliant teacher who had encouraged them to be independent and to utilize their scientific knowledge. They knew how to read the ancient boulders and rocks that kept their secrets hidden for millions of years. They spread out over the lava rock, kicking stones, as they searched out a particular ledge here and there. Often, they squinted at the unrecognizable, hoping to see hidden secrets that predated even the Jurassic. They spent several days searching the rock outcroppings, sharing their finds, and documenting their days' work.

15. Paul

ONE OF THE MORE FASTIDIOUS of the students was a young man from Wyoming by the name of Paul. He was no stranger to geology, having spent much of his youth in the outdoors of his home state of Montana with his family on fishing and hunting excursions. He had grown to love the mountains, often hiking forbidden trails. As he matured, he spent many hours rock climbing on even the most challenging mountains, including Devil's Tower. These minor feats he added to a fast-developing resume, and he was already showing much promise as his teacher's prized pupil.

As the students continued with their daily work of shoveling and sifting through the debris of time, Paul had become particularly interested in one sight. The first couple of days he spent moving around from one outcropping to another, working meticulously with hammer and brushes. He immersed himself in trying to cover as much territory as possible without overlooking any clues. Often he grew frustrated with the chippings and dust, but he persevered in his quest, knowing that eventually the rocks would yield to him.

Their last day was Sunday. All had arisen as early as possible, so as not to miss the various stages of daybreak, as shadows often could hide major finds. They had set off in earnest, walking along the trail that they had worn into the side of the plateau where they had been working. Paul returned to the site that had gathered his interest on the previous afternoon. Today he decided that the particular outcropping had more than a fleeting interest to him; there was something unusual about the setting and the obliqueness of the rocks themselves. He arrived at the site, a good thirty yards from the others, and began to laboriously explore. He was fastidious, almost studious, in his undertaking, being careful not to disturb the site or to make it unrecognizable. He carefully started his dredging movement. Using his skills and patience, he scratched and clawed until his hand was able to feel an odd horizontal line.

Slowly, the labors started to take on meaning; he started to see the beginning of a large, fissure-like opening. The length could not be determined from where he was positioned; it was strictly guesswork at this point. He stood up and slowly backed away from his diggings, trying to objectively size up the area. He squinted into the sun and was unable to get the fissure's true dimensions, so again he returned to his work and began to dig further into the site.

Kirk watched the students with a watchful, paternalistic eye as they worked nearby, all consumed with studying the formations of epochs that had long ago made their marks on an ever-changing planet. He was now watching with a little more interest the progress that Paul had been making. Through the early hours of the morning up until the afternoon, he had noticed the frenetic pace his student had taken in the rock outcroppings. Now at his position Kirk was able to view the beginnings of a division in the rock. He made out the faint beginnings of the fissure but also what appeared to be a layering and separation that was running horizontally in an east-west orientation. The total effect was similar to a fault line. Kirk's trained eyes gave him the capability to observe the obscure and subtle clues that could so easily be overlooked by a less trained eye. He watched intently as the student continued on with his methodical work, deciding not to disturb Paul as he kept at his digging. Kirk followed Paul's progress as the day wore on and began to see that this was going to be a significant find that would require more than a casual few days away from the classroom. Paul too, was beginning to see the rewards of his work; he suspected that what he had unearthed might possibly be the beginnings of a cavern, but the indentation was more of a separation or layering of rock against rock. At this point the fissure's true length, depth, and other statistics could not fully be measured; Paul needed the expertise of his professor.

Paul was about to leave the site when Kirk approached him. He knew at that point that his work was being followed. Questions were beginning to form in his mind when his teacher told him that the site was unique and that more time and study would be required in order to fully appreciate what he had uncovered. With the help of the other students, they set about taking measurements of the site and surveying what they could. The primary concern after all their days of work was the fault-like angles and layering that appeared to be so pervasive even in the infancy of the excavation. They needed to view the site from a distance in order to see if it was truly a fault line or just erosion, which was found in so many of the ancient outcroppings in the area.

To the northeast of them were the towns near Grand Coulee. The same geographical fingers that had formed the area's hills, plateaus, and canyons were all prevalent in the rough architecture they surveyed. The dam itself was welded into these very same monoliths of prehistory, unmoved by man's tools and answering only to the whispers of time and the subtle movements of tectonic plates. The students knew they needed to answer many more questions in regard to their outing in the very near future.

16. Electric City

To Electric City, the dam was as grand as its name. It was a functioning giant, complete and colossal. It meant tourism and security. It was photographed and revered as well as providing the millions and billions of gallons of water that had given a great desert the opportunity to provide sustenance for its peoples. It had provided the town with employment and security as well as a light show at night. Those who lived there never tired of her massive concrete walls with their water rushing over spillways almost five hundred feet to the river floor. The dam had set the pace for the town for almost sixty years and would keep on doing so for hundreds more. The people of Electric City were proud of their dam; they bragged about it, spoke of its attributes, and pointed their fingers to it as though it was a concrete icon.

Most important, they never tired of it. They felt so privileged in having such a large neighbor in their very backyards that they never considered it a risk.

Kirk and his pupils had returned to Ellensburg and the CWU campus; they were a little tired but also a little excited. They were still pondering the results of Paul's find in the cliffs above Lake Roosevelt. Kirk was perplexed. His main concern was how to approach the problem, what resources would be needed, and where would the moneys come from to provide the in-depth examination that would be required to evaluate the site thoroughly. Kirk's find would be important, as they all knew in part the ramifications of a possible fault line.

Kirk was not long in starting his networking with old geological cronies and others familiar with the area that they had been excavating. He knew that he must have hard facts in front of him if there would be any hope in lining up college moneys or other sources of funding. He had been back from the site for several days and was more perplexed with the problem than he had been at its inception. His primary concern was obvious to him: how long was the fissure, and was it a fault or just an anomaly in the rock itself? The days that followed found him poring over old pictures of the area pictures as well as information regarding the building of the dam with photographs showing the strata and geological makeup of the area prior to the construction of the dam. Kirk spent many hours scrutinizing the photos, often with magnifying glass, hoping to discover some subtle crease or signature of the shifting of the earth. His efforts were not rewarded; there was nothing to be seen in the photos.

By the end of the week, Kirk had grown frustrated with his search. If he had proof of previous movements in rock, there would be no concern in regard to the stability of the area. But he had no answers, only questions, and was dissatisfied with the end result of his tedious detective work. The site would have to be visually and manually gone over, a process that demanded not only skilled manpower and energy but also utilization of the scientific process. His next trip over to the basin would also call for money.

Kirk was as resilient as he was resourceful. With the tenacity of a bulldog, he began a process of working the phone and seeking out those who might contribute to his cause. His search took him throughout the state, often ending in blind leads. Eventually he began to touch on a few enterprising souls who were truly interested in his cause. In some instances, there was a small hitch: they wanted to come along. Kirk also was able to pull some of the grant moneys out of his department as well as talk another department head into a loan provided that he gave him a promissory note in return. This was a highly unusual ploy, but his colleague was more than a little interested in the project.

Kirk had spent at least a couple of weeks rounding up finances to fund the work, he also had to get permits and deal with other assorted items of state bureaucracy in order to justify his curiosity. Finally, he had the university to convince. He went before everyone from the regents to the provost and finally the president himself. In the end he had convinced all that his was a worthy cause.

The spring rains fell steady now on the Northwest. They were subtle, gradually filling lakes and rivers that had already swelled with the melting winter's snows. Rivers moved more swiftly, lakes lapped high upon the shore, and the people in the bigger cities grew aggravated with continuous rains. April would soon become May. Farmers who often worried about drought were now faced with flooded fields, and they looked at overcast skies with threatening storm clouds and hoped for relief.

17. Jake and Keith

The Hendersons had seen more than enough rain and snow to last them a lifetime. Jake and Keith were now spending long days trying to rectify the damages done by the persistent storms. A good part of the day was spent on the four-wheeler, going from ditch to ditch and shoveling in the hopes of guiding the irrigation waters handily on their way. The brothers were consumed with worry about drowning their crops. They had planted earlier, but they were in doubt about any future success. The fields were often muck, fit only for a rice paddy. They fought the mud daily, shoveling and reopening ditches that had blocked up on their own. This was now a daily ordeal.

The evenings were quiet. They would reflect on the day's toils, often sitting quietly or going outside to have a smoke and gaze at fields that were dormant but hopefully would provide the essence of a livelihood. Casper, through all of his convalescence, was able to see the wear and tear the farm was subjecting his sons to. He himself had seen all the obstacles a hard winter and spring could provide, and he also knew that whatever destiny would provide was out of his hands. He often would listen intently to his sons' conversations for some indication that they would not be defeated by the whims of the weather. Rubbing at a day's growth of grizzled beard, he said nothing, sat quietly, and often stared at the empty fields.

The routine started to wear a little too much on the brothers. As spring edged closer toward summer, they often would take a break from the daily chores and aggravation to head to town for beer and relaxation. They never really had an agenda to follow other than finding a relaxing corner of the local bar and watching the action as their neighbors slowly came in from the toils of their fields to throw back beer and tell a few tales. They often hit town during early sunset. With the springtime weather moving beyond April, they began to see a little relief from the rains. The sun was a little warmer, and this proved to be a more sociable time of year. Area farmers had spent much of the fall and winter sticking close to home, but now they were able to come into town and enjoy each other's company, get drunk together, and even have a few fights if that was part of the night's activities.

Jake looked for any excuse to get to town after he began seeing Nora. Often she would be bartending or waitressing at the single café/bar in town. She was always stunning as far as Jake was concerned; he enjoyed her company. She was an easy woman, not in the sense of creatures of the night but compassionate and open, with just enough sophistication and mystique to pique Jake's interest. So the trips to town after the farming came with a little more regularity, and so did the hangovers. More than once the brothers would stay till closing time before heading home, and often Keith was the only one who left. Jake stayed on with Nora.

18. Chris and Bonneville

Chris spent a sleepless night. His thoughts were on chaos—and not just any run-of-the-mill chaos, but the type that caused whole systems to close down and shutter, the type that could bring entire governments to their knees with the planting of one small virus. No wonder they gave the name "virus" to the computer plants that ran amok and erased entire systems; it was an appropriate name that fit right in with technological vocabularies. Chris was excited. He had been toying a little more with various entries into some key government bodies, and he was able to circumnavigate their security systems and leave his calling cards. Obviously he was an unwanted intruder, but he was oblivious to the risks of getting caught, so he decided to take his exploits up another notch.

He settled on April 15, 1999, for his next plot. He waited throughout the morning and afternoon that day for the time of day when traffic would be heaviest on the net. He picked the hours between 6:00 and 8:00 p.m. when many would be involved in their daily routines, searching for everything from stock market results to their favorite porn sites. The traffic was always heavy at that time, and on some days it was much heavier than others. He knew that after logging on he would be able to maintain a certain degree of obscurity, analogous to being lost in the crowd. In the relative silence of his home, he typed in his commands and requests, waited as passwords were recognized, and then began his work effortlessly and surreptitiously. He keyed in the sought-out search, and after a few moments the screen revealed the words "BPA" and then "power grid." Chris smiled and then as an afterthought pumped his fist into the air, almost in a victory sign.

The Bonneville dam was one of the first dams built on the Columbia. It was also the first of a succession of dams that moved in an easterly fashion until heading due north at the Snake River junction. It had seen much history. Barges and other river navigators had long used its locks to traffic in their daily imports and exports as those heading west headed for the open Pacific and the Orient beyond. Heading east were the towns of Lewiston and Clarkston, part of an inland empire that gave way to the opening of that part of the Northwest in regard to commerce and progress. It was an aging edifice, lackluster but maintained, its fish ladders almost vacant from the once-thriving times of the Steelhead and Chinook salmon, so many that even those who had the mundane job of counting them found it strenuous. Now the Bonneville, like the dams above it, seldom counted the salmon that were fast disappearing from the old spawning grounds, largely because of the dams that blocked their way.

The men who worked on the Bonneville dam were well aware of the controversies being contested by various groups concerned with the vanishing salmon. The salmon had been a mainstay of the tourist industry as well as a boost to the fishing industry, and with the relative overnight success of Seattle becoming one of the most livable cities of the late 1980s and 90s, philosophies changed. The outside influx of people moving to the Northwest brought their own ideas and beliefs on what should happen to the Columbia.

There had been proposals of removing the dams and the locks so the Columbia could again flow unrestricted. The first of the dams mentioned for removal was the Bonneville. It was a project that the Army Corps of Engineers was none too eager to tackle in the future.

19. The Grid Responds

ON THE DRIZZLY DAY OF April 16, the dam stood quietly, not all of its spillways open the Columbia that flowed quietly and serenely behind it. The various workers who toiled daily outside of her as well as inside methodically did their jobs. Groundskeepers manicured the lawns in the tourist area, saw that garbage was picked up, and carefully made last-minute adjustments to picnic areas before the first tours made their way through the visitors' area. Inside the various control panels were watched closely as electricity was generated and sent on its way through the power lines that fed into the large transformers. The day began innocently enough. Nobody was really mindful of the dam itself; it was almost as if it didn't exist. It was there, but its purpose was not equated with the vast jobs of navigation and electricity generation it performed as well as employing the many men who daily worked in and on her grounds. Halfway through the morning, while workers were engrossed in their tasks, the first of the mammoth spillways slowly, effortlessly, began to slide along its track. Immediately, the river behind began to eagerly cascade through the offered opening. Almost silently, the several other spillways began to open, offering the pent-up Columbia her freedom and the Pacific beyond.

Alarms began to go off immediately in and around the dam. Those who lived upriver could hear the warnings but were unaware of the problems that now occupied those who manned the dam. Bonneville employees found themselves in a quandary when the first of the gates began to open. They watched helplessly as water poured over the spillway. They asked each other if they had missed a directive or a memo that would have informed them of this, but their stares only were met with the blank expressions of their colleagues. In the control arena of the Bonneville Dam, the technicians and engineers watched unwittingly as their gauges and various computers and screens flashed and bleeped insanely, there was an air of fear and apprehension as the systems took on a life of their own. The technicians, gate controllers, and other assorted professionals tried to reestablish the normalcy that had started out the morning.

At BPA in Portland, the chaos downstream had not escaped the upper crust of management. The uncanny events had started a cascade of consequences that continued throughout the day. The Army Corps of Engineers and other government agencies were all notified of the event as it unfolded, though they would have found out soon enough anyway. Technicians began searching for some errant command responsible for the problems they were facing. They downloaded systems that could have been responsible for the opening of the spillways, and they were also concerned about a replication in dams that were upriver. The entire process was tedious and maddening, but the men worked diligently to find the answer.

Dave had also spent the entire morning searching his banks of information. He began to suspect that the morning's activities were related to the glitch he had recently encountered. His search had previously come up empty handed, but he had spent time alerting other BPA officials of the anomalies and documented them. Now his concern was more of an act of desperation as he too sought to find what had caused so much confusion as to render a great river helpless. He spent much of the morning himself downloading information, troubleshooting with the other technicians, and searching throughout the power grid, hoping to find whatever had caused the problem. All the while, his subconscious was telling him, *hacker, hacker*. Where did the virus start, and was it replicating?

At Bonneville the confusion and alarms had kept a steady pace since the gates had first opened. Navigation had come to a standstill, and all matter of routine daily activities had been canceled. There was grave concern inside the controls of the dam as communications were relayed back and forth to Portland; much energy had been expended in the day's frustrations. Portland was at a loss, and those who worked on the dam had a feeling of helplessness as they watched millions of gallons of water seek the spillways and beyond. In Portland, downriver, another plan was starting to go into play: a possible escape route for floods if the need materialized. At the early planning stage, the problem seemed overwhelming, and the prospect of evacuating almost a million souls seemed hopeless.

On top of the dam, men milled about monitoring the event as it unfolded. They watched throughout the day, hoping that technology would somehow stay the flow of water and spray. At approximately 5:00 p.m., the first of the giant spillways slowly closed. Within minutes, as if by silent command, the other spillways closed in quiet succession.

The river below took on a calm innocence as the raging water again was quieted; the hour of the day was noted for future reference. Those who worked on the dam sighed in collective relief. Below the dam, the million or more souls that lived in and around Portland had no idea of the possible calamity that would have befallen them until the following days. Area newspapers would release the story over a period of days, and the nightly news would inundate the airwaves for several days after. To the men who had witnessed the unleashing of the Columbia, many questions would follow as news media sought answers themselves and asked if greater dangers would follow. These were just a few of the myriad of questions that were being posed by the population below Bonneville. After a period of several days, calm began to return along with normalcy. The media continued their ongoing barrage of questions and concerns but sought the middle ground rather than operating with an air of accusation and paranoia. The nation watched from a safe distance as officials sought to rectify or justify that unusual day when in a worst-case scenario the entire city of Portland and surrounding communities could have been submerged like an Atlantis under several feet of water.

Chris lounged comfortably in his dad's lazy boy. It was Saturday morning, and he was reading the *Seattle Post Intelligencer*. He didn't have to look far for what he was seeking; it had made the front pages of not only local papers but those all over the nation. He had a smirk on his face as he engrossed himself in the article pertaining to the incident at the Bonneville Dam, all that power and those raging waters unleashed by the simple strokes of a keyboard. He was demonic in his need to fulfill himself with further excursions on the Internet to see what other targets he could break into, so in the solitude of his parents' home he spent the rest of the day considering his future. He was carefully considering the options available. He knew that if he proceeded with further moves, he would be pursued. Every major government agency, from the FBI to local law authorities, would seek him out. He decided to briefly put an end to his crime spree, the rest of the afternoon was spent downloading incriminating evidence and destroying other personal data in order to be prepared if the authorities eventually found him out. He decided that his capture would be tantamount at this juncture, and he knew how to destroy the errant software, after all. In the end he would have an encore, but for now the project was on the back burner.

Billy spent the afternoon of April 17 in town. He had gone in with a friend to get a few groceries and run some errands when he heard the news about the Bonneville Dam. The story didn't affect his routine. It was a lazy Saturday afternoon, the news said only that the matter was being investigated. He felt that whoever was involved with the mess wasn't saying too much; it was better to have the public ignorant of something that could do so much damage, causing flooding, loss of life, and whatever else could happen. He thought about the river in a reflective mood. After all, it was in his own front yard, not more than a mile from his home. No matter where you lived on the Columbia, if it was low ground there was always danger of flooding.

Billy and his friend finished up their business in town and made the drive back to Schawana. The trip back was not without celebration. Billy once again had broken his abstinence, so they found a couple out-of-the-way taverns and filled their trip with spirit. Eventually they made it back without being arrested. They talked briefly about the previous day, but neither wanted to dwell on something so ominous as the potential of the Columbia River.

20. Ned

In Kettle Falls, Ned found himself getting ready for the upcoming summer. All around his compound were various tasks to keep him busy, and every passing year there seemed to be more to do than in the year preceding it. The cabins were in need of repainting, and many of the indoor fixtures needed repair or replacement. He was more inclined at this juncture to look for a buyer but felt he would stay with the enterprise for now. When he heard about the Bonneville dam, he was a little miffed. He often wondered about some kind of calamity or natural disaster hitting his niche of the world. After all, he was at the head of one of the vastest manmade lakes in the country, and with all the dams that stopped the river's flow, he often found himself thinking about what could happen in a similar situation. He began to hear local gossip as the days following the near catastrophe passed. What he heard disturbed him, but he chose not to become involved with the talk. Rather, he listened.

As was his usual routine, he again began taking his walks by the lake. He scratched vigorously at two days' growth of beard; he chose not to shave when his wife was out of town. As he plodded along the water's edge, he looked outward toward the vast blueness of the lake. It was dotted with boats that at his vantage point were small dots on the horizon, almost insignificant. His aging eyes searched the calm with persistence, hoping to reveal some chink or clue that would reveal a weakness in the topography of the lake. He was dogged in this ambition, pushed on by all the recent newspaper articles and his own need to have answers to all his questions.

At length he would find he had no solution to all his nagging intuitiveness. The lake was peaceful, silent, and strong. He watched at length the boaters who were closer to shore plying the waves with skillfulness and abandon. Ned stopped, picked up a rock, and slowly returned to the azure water. He watched long after as the ripples silently fanned out from where the rock had made its entrance. Then, with a moment of respectful hesitation, he finally turned and quietly made his way back to the cabins. Ned had suspicions; he had a long history of living so close to the same lake that had provided him with security, with bounty for his family and the home that had provided for his wife and children until the children were finally adults and able to move on independently with their own lives. He had viewed this world on a daily basis over decades; he had watched its ebbs and flows, its silent lapping at the shore, and its highs and lows, and never had he felt the concern that had plodded at him now as he surveyed the glassy waters. He took one last glance and then returned back to the cabins.

21. The Alarmists

KIRK HAD A GO; HE had been able to procure the blessings of college administration, from the president on down. He was giddy with the results and even happier with how he was able to get the funding necessary to pursue what he had already perceived as a major find. The rest of April and well into May he spent gathering all the necessary resources together. He decided to wait until the spring quarter had ended before actually throwing himself into the undertaking. He knew that during final exams and the marking period, his time would be too compromised to give the project the attention it would demand.

Kirk started off briskly. After he had secured the necessary funds and had cut through all the bureaucratic paperwork, he was able to focus on who would be involved with the work. The whole process did not go without glitches: as part of his application process, he encountered roadblocks that he was not prepared for. The primary one was of tribal rights and burial grounds. He and some of his more knowledgeable cronies in the end were able to establish with local tribes in their area of work that they would not disturb the spirits at rest. This required much documentation and gathered oral history of the area, and they felt relieved when they finally got the okay from tribal elders. After the burial ground hurdle was cleared, there were a few environmental issues to clear with state, county, and local politicos as well as the usual environmental impact studies. Kirk was able to clear these as well. Throughout his years he had well established a proficient network that reached all the way to the top: favors returned for favors given. The project was now ready to begin.

Kirk began in earnest. He found himself quibbling over whom he would invite and whom he would be leaving behind. He already had a rough idea of which graduate students would be coming along; obviously it would be his most dedicated and promising students. Those included Paul, whom he had already held in high esteem. At times he saw in his ambitious student a little of himself, and although he did not covet his skills he found himself often a little envious. With the end of the quarterly studies, Kirk began the process of notifying the handpicked grad students as well as letting some of the individual investors/adventurers know the start date and timeframe of setting up. This was no minor matter, as it took the better part of two weeks to get their supplies, tools, transportation, and technological support into place. When the day of departure came, it was with glee that the assorted students, teachers, and others found themselves luxuriating in what might feasibly change the course of geology in the area of their conquest.

At the University of Washington in late April, the campus took on the airs of spring. Students greeted each other on the walkways as they hurried toward their respective classes. It was a time of renewal, and youthful ambitions were reinvented with the departure from a long and wet winter. In the one building on the campus that pursued the interest of geology and volcanology, as well as other aspects of the natural world, the spring phenomenon was not shared. Kirk had recently been in touch with old friends in that department and by phone had briefed them on their finds in the basin. That did not set off bells and whistles, but no find or even a hint of a find goes unnoticed. These were professionals well aware of nature unleashed in all its monstrosity; all they had to do was remind themselves of Mt. Saint Helens and the other sleeping giants up and down the Cascade chain. So with the respect due any credible colleague, they began to pursue leads that were in the vicinity of Kirk's find.

They began with enthusiasm. Recently there had been some minor movements in the continental shelves in the Pacific. The movements were always suspect, as you had great tectonic plates moving or sliding over each other. This was always watched carefully, as the whole West Coast was often perceived to be in perpetual danger as these events came about. There was always much apprehension, but rather than proceeding when nature made its overtures, the specialists spent most of their days and nights carefully analyzing their graphs, charts, and seismographs in order to allay any fears before ringing the alarmist's bells. The West and the Northwest was still in their infancy: as geological clocks go, they were a work in progress, with numerous earthquakes in California as well as the volcanoes in Washington State, which formed what many call the Pacific Rim of Fire. When Kirk had displayed some urgency in his conversations to his scientist friends, the message did not fall on deaf ears.

While his request for more technological assistance on the site was being actively assessed and researched by his cronies at the U. of W., Kirk busied himself with the formalities of getting ready for the departure. He already had hand picked the grad students who were going to accompany him as well as a few others who were going along for the ride, primarily friends who had opened up their checkbooks to him and had their own agendas to fulfill. Their outing promised to be of significance in the world of geology, and although it was being kept quiet, there had been some leaks and a little more attention than necessary. With everything a go, Kirk made the decision to leave in late June.

22. Plates Moving

SEVERAL DAYS HAD PROCEEDED ALONG without anything concrete. Data were interpreted and reinterpreted, looking for clues. It happened subtly in early morning hours while many were still sleeping. One of the grad students, while watching offshore movement, discovered what looked like a long rift almost imperceptible to the naked eye. He carefully noted the location and looked for similar movements off the coast but did not see any indication of movement with the exception of what he was now looking at. He made a few phone calls and found out that there had been some minor earthquake activity over in the basin area.

The following day, the student corralled some of his superiors to discuss the findings. They were always interested in any new findings, especially in regard to quake activity. They reviewed the information provided by the grad student but saw something more crucial than what the student had provided. In looking at graphs of data from the area, they were able to discern older activity in the basin area around Lake Roosevelt going in a northeastern direction. It appeared that the newer activity had connected up at a juncture that paralleled the older rift as if forming an unbroken seam, with the bulk of activity a few kilometers away from Kirk's camp. They wasted no time before alerting Kirk of their find.

Kirk was even more excited after receiving the information. He knew that in the weeks following his return other researchers would be busy scouring the area looking for other signs of activity, and what they found might well be extremely important. After making a few checks on equipment and personnel, Kirk made arrangements to leave over the course of the next few days. Everything and everybody was in readiness to go.

Dave had been burned out with the recent events at Bonneville. He had spent almost every waking hour diligently pursuing leads in order to find the virus and its origins, but this proved to be futile. He had thought that over a period of time some leads would turn up, but whoever had so insidiously placed them had somehow escaped their expertise. The perpetrator had to be someone very knowledgeable who knew how to escape detection as if vanishing off the face of the earth. There had not been any further incidents of spillways opening up without the proper channels, but still, someone was out there and could again leave an entire power structure as well as navigation at risk. The culprit left a virus but nothing indicating who he was.

23. A Camping Trip

DAVE WAS ALSO HAVING PROBLEMS with his ex. He had been to court with his lawyer, ironing out technical details in terms of support and visitation. This was taking its toll on his work as well as what little social life he was having. He decided to put in for a few well-deserved vacation days to at least rejuvenate himself and get a better perspective on his life. He was able to get his boss to let him take a long weekend. His boss knew that Dave was having difficulty with past marital obligations, and along with the other stresses with recent events, he felt that one of his more valued employees would benefit from the brief hiatus. He gave Dave his blessings and sent him out the door.

At home that evening, Dave was in a reflective spirit. He felt his head clearing from the enormity of his past stresses, marital and work related. He felt a sense of glee and giddiness that he had not felt for some time. He decided to call the ex, and after finding her in a relatively calm demeanor, he went ahead and asked her to let his boys come along on his brief vacation. She acquiesced, and at that he felt he was batting a thousand. Not only was he able to convince his boss to give him vacation, he was also able to wrangle his kids free from their mother's apron strings. Eureka!

He packed up some camping supplies that evening. He really had no set agenda as far as destination went, but he wanted it to be outside; after all, he had the entire Pacific Northwest at his disposal. He checked through all his camping gear to make sure he had a tent that was leak-free as well as sleeping bags, a Coleman stove, and a few fishing poles. He felt ready for the great outdoors, a novice woodsman.

The following morning he went to a nearby convenience store and stocked up on a few essentials for the great camping excursion, making sure that he had all the sundry items necessary to keep an adult along with his two boys well provided for while camping. There were plenty of hot dogs, bacon, eggs, and ice for the cooler, which was already stocked with beer and pop. He left the store feeling like a new man with a fresh purchase on life, an explorer seeking out new adventures with his progeny. He made the quick drive up the highway to his old home and found the boys ready to go. They were out of school, so the trip couldn't have been at a better time. Their mother was also there to meet him; she had already taken her stance on the threshold and gave Dave a long list of dos and don'ts with respect to the boys' welfare. Dave was really too oblivious to hear any of the parting orders; he was too overwhelmed by the sheer luck of having the boys for several days to really consume what his wife had said. After her soliloquy about what he had to do, he watched as she hugged them and returned back to her domain inside. He felt like giving her the finger but thought better of it; perchance she would happen to see the explicit gesture and forever prohibit him from seeing his children again.

They started out relatively early, as they wanted to get a good piece of roadway behind them before dark. They decided they would only have to stop for gas and the usual rest stops; they could always raid the cooler, which had more than enough provisions to keep them fueled. Before leaving and picking up his boys, Dave had taken a cursory look at one of his road maps and decided that a trip along the Columbia might be interesting. After all, he had been up that way before and found it to be scenic. As far as a destination he was still unsure, but he felt confident that he and the boys would be able to decide on something. By midday they had covered a couple hundred miles. Instead of taking a route via the Dalles and heading into Washington, they found themselves following the river. After all, they might run into some great fishing along its shores at some obscure campsite. Instead, they put more miles behind them, almost lost in a hypnotic trance of suggestion as they found themselves turning northward and moving on.

Life was starting to become more purposeful as the guys found themselves venturing farther and farther up the highway. They had begun their cruise on 84 East, and well into the trip they made the curve toward Pasco via Wallula, a short skip and a jump. In a sense it was big country, dotted with sagebrush here and there, but acres of golden wheat also stretched as far as the eye could see. Everything about this part of the state of Washington was big and empty. They didn't mind the emptiness; it was part of their as-yet-to-be-determined destination. They were adventurers on a mission. So they kept at it, picking up

182 and following the Columbia, a mighty blue snake, as she meandered northward toward Canada. They hit several small towns on their trip, all of them along the river and with nothing more than a small grocery store and gas station. They were places like Mattawa, Schawana, and Beverly, hot and arid towns looking for some promise of prosperity and finding none.

They continued on, the weather had been promising from the beginning, early-summer hot. They decided to cut across I-90 toward Quincy and then to Soap Lake and beyond. Finally, toward the end of their day they decided to do the tourist thing and stop off at Grand Coulee Dam. Their trip for the most part had been uneventful, with the exception of what travelers see while moving across a state. They had stopped off at the occasional vista points and surveyed volcanic cliffs and sheer drops down to the waiting river below. They had also seen a few overheated cars and cursing, out-of-state motorists short on patience but long on disgust. Toward their first major stop they were slowed by several vehicles that were going in their direction. Several young and middle-aged men stood around on the shoulder of the road, looking at various maps and checking out one of the vehicles that appeared to have broken down. Dave decided to stop, as the group looked benign, almost academic. They offered assistance and were welcomed by what seemed to be the leader of this motley crew—Kirk, as Dave remembered it, who said something about geological survey in the area. They spent enough time to exchange a few good-natured helloes and find out that no assistance was needed. Then they moved on down the highway.

Dave secretly and subconsciously had wanted to see the dam; the idea had been in the back of his mind long before he had started off with his boys on their excursion. He spent sleepless nights thinking about the problems encountered at Bonneville and the uncaught hacker responsible. His dreams lead him up a much-harnessed river, peaceful and yet capable of defiance.

He thought about the many obstacles placed on her in order to exploit and tame as well as navigate her. So the pure order of her led up through the maze of dams that crossed her width, slowing down the Columbia, until at the end of this puzzle stood the jewel in its crown, the Grand Coulee Dam, a monolith of gray concrete as much alive as inanimate. Dave was to see it for the very first time in his life.

They came on 174, not pushing the speed limit as this was no superhighway. Signs and mile markers all indicated that they were getting a little closer to the manmade wonder of the world. When finally they had crept up behind her, as if stalking some large, ferocious animal, they noticed the mile or so width of her yaw. Then they saw the peeking of sunlight through her spillways, all eleven, and the course of the river as its currents made individual drops. Finally they were in front and watching as the Columbia coursed through the dam and its arteries: a magnificent sight. Water foamed down several hundred feet to the surface below and then onward. Dave and his boys sought out another vantage point in order to fully appreciate the wonder of it all and take a few snapshots; they found a perfect spot for this and were not alone. They studied its front, and Dave gauged its immensity with careful precision less he lose some small aspect of its strength and beauty. His eyes followed the full breadth and height of the dam from one end to another, stopping at the third power house. When constructed in the late sixties and early seventies, it had given even more electricity to the very same grid he worked for. All around him and his children were other tourists, all oohing and aahing at this marvel of engineering. Yet as intrigued as Dave was about the dam's mastery, he also was a little bit apprehensive. He pushed a week's worth of worry about the river and its fragility to the back of his mind.

Dave and his kids spent the remainder of the day searching for a decent hotel room in the area. There was the usual pick of them, and most had vacancies, as the tourist season was not quite in full swing. They settled on a little mom-and-pop that put them within a few miles of the dam. They had decided earlier to forego camping, as the hour was late and setting up in the darkness would prove to be a hassle. Besides that, they were too worn out for the physical requirements of pitching a camp. They checked into their room, stowed their belongings, cleaned up a little, and headed off to a nearby drive-in. They ate burgers and fries before taking one last look at Grand Coulee in the evening. Then they headed back to their room and the luxury of a good night's sleep.

Morning came early, and they were ready to go with the first light. They drove into Electric City, filled up on hotcakes, and then were on the road, pointing in a northerly direction. The road they traveled ended up taking them to Kettle Falls. Along the way they followed Lake Roosevelt. Its size was almost incomprehensible; its width was almost greater than the eye could measure. They enjoyed their trip, and when they had finally reached their destination they found a campground that still had a few openings. They were not far from Ned's cabins, and after getting into the campground they were able to locate a site, park, and begin the task of setting up the tent and all the prerequisites involved in roughing it in the wild.

24. SRI

SATELLITES WOUND THEIR PREDESTINED PATHS hundreds of miles above the blue planet. They were not visible during the day, but sometimes at night if one was lucky, a glimpse could be made of their circling. At one point only one or two had been launched into the stratosphere. By the eighties and nineties, the hundreds that at any given time circled the globe almost created traffic congestion. It was and is no secret what their agendas are; they are the secret eyes of warring countries trying to gain the unfair advantage from their lofty places above. In their ranks, all types of information is gathered, from the movement of militaries to snowstorms. The gathering tools and cameras of one particular satellite were able to zoom in on an earthquake hundreds of miles below as it careened through the waters of Washington and finally rolled inland, to no apparent repercussion except a 5.5 on the Richter scale at Golden, Colorado.

The information soon found its way to the geology labs at UW. The wonks in the lab itself grew more ecstatic as the information came into them via their screens and assorted monitors, all strategically placed throughout the building. It was now June, a time when classrooms were vacant and students were gone. The solitude on the campus grounds did not extend to the labs, where dozens of teachers, grad students, and assorted others stood, tediously analyzing every bit of information as it materialized.

Their interests became apparent as the day lengthened. Some new information gave even more latitude to the information already gathered: a little-known secret called SRI, or Synthetic Radar Imaging, a concept that was seeing new applications from mining to seeking temples in overgrown rain forests. With this science the guys in the lab were able to make their image of the quake into a three-dimensional picture. They were in awe. They could see not only see past rifts but also the here and now. With this recent quake they saw some new risks, many in the area where their colleague and friend was now exploring in the basin. They had images only; they now sought hard evidence. They wasted no time in contacting Kirk.

In the field, Kirk was a maverick and tenacious as a bulldog. He never gave in and oftentimes found himself at odds with students and peers alike. His methods were straightforward: keep going until you find what you are looking for, and don't leave until the hard facts are in hand. It was this philosophy that gained him the respect, as well as the notoriety, he deserved—and often times the envy of his ilk. His trip to the basin had been a secretive one. Only a select few were knowledgeable about the ramifications of what he sought. There was a great deal of optimism that fueled the group, but Kirk and Kirk only knew the full extent of what he hoped to find. The entire group wasted no effort in regards to technology. All were armed with all the recent toys, including laptops, cell phones, and anything else needed to make sure that any new information was relayed immediately and without a hitch.

Kirk had recently received the communiqué from Seattle via his laptop. He had a mock campsite and was not committed to setting up any campsite until he had a chance to review and analyze all the latest developments flowing to him from his colleagues across the Cascades. He capitalized on the experience of his team. All were well versed in their prospective fields, and all were young enough to withstand the rigors of the field. The team spent a fortnight in their makeshift campsite. Kirk had given all a briefing on the new information about the recent earthquake as well as problem areas that they would be looking for. As for the updated material concerning SRI, Kirk saved that tidbit for himself. He knew that in the end these data, as well as the physical evidence from their expedition, could be used to corroborate their findings. He wanted no premature leaks and trusted no one until the time was right.

On day two, the entire team got their equipment together. They had stayed over at a site in the Soap Lake area, a ramshackle town hard in the basin with a brief history of tourists coming to soak in the lake's curative waters in search of some sort of cure from imagined or real ailments. The town had a few inhabitants, and in the summer when the sun beat down relentlessly the only signs of life were those few thirsty souls who sought relief in the two or three taprooms that could be found on the main street. It was fitting that Kirk and his peers started out on their excavations from a place of such obscurity. They left early in the morning, well stocked in provisions and familiar with the topography that they would soon be exploring. They were not far from the site itself. Their previous expedition was only a few kilometers from the actual site of the recent findings of activity via satellite. Their new camp would be within a mile or so of where they planned to set up. They wanted to be close but have enough margin of error so as to not disturb any potential findings.

They arrived at 8:30 a.m. Already the air shimmered with the promise of a hot day and no relief from the sun. There was little shade to be found. They began the tasks of setting up a base camp. Each man was given a specific job, whether it was setting up their electronics equipment or scouting out the area for other promising finds. The day casually descended into the evening hours. Life at the camp grew into a succession of ramblings and pep talks as the men worked through the hours of getting equipment set up and focusing on the days ahead. Kirk sat quietly in his tent, poring over all the recent e-mails and assorted technical advice. He knew that within a short distance of the campsite, a major rift was occurring. All that was needed now was for him to bring back the physical evidence. He was more than ready for the conquest.

25. A Fishing Trip

JAKE SAT QUIETLY ON THE porch, deep in thought about the future of the farm. They were in hock with the bank, and so far, the crops that they had sown were not fulfilling their promise. They struggled day in and day out, and the future would have to change if the family was to ever realize a profit and a productive farm. The old man wasn't much help either; he had recovered from his stroke but was often flying off the handle for the most trivial of events. He would often pace around the house forgetting where he had put assorted personal items and spend hours rummaging and cursing to no one in particular. The change became apparent soon after his recovery process began. It was more noticeable now, and the old man was also given to crying jags and not knowing what the cause was. The two younger men decided that it was all part of the stroke, and they did what they could to console him and include him as much as possible in any plans that involved the farm. They did this, though, with hesitation.

June crept by at length. The only real excitement in the area was some small aftershocks that were the result of an earthquake that was centered farther up the river. Jake did not seem overly concerned with this; he only felt it odd that an earthquake would be in this area. The only major geologic catastrophes had been St. Helens and the movement of huge glaciers thousands of years ago. The only perceptible signs were the behavior of the livestock and the dog. All seemed out of sorts and jittery for several days after the actual quake. Jake was a little perplexed by all of the natural phenomena and couldn't help but feel an uncanny queasiness, almost like dread. In spite of all the new events in their lives, they had no time to analyze nature's fury and focused more on the farm.

During late June, the brothers busied themselves around the farm. There was no shortage of chores to fulfill. Several of their fences were in disrepair, and many of the outbuildings needed some patching and roof repair. In mid-June they were almost ready to get in their second cutting of hay. They soon would be back out in the fields in early morning and late afternoon with the swather and baler. They looked at the month as more promising than the previous spring months, when all they had was the threat of constant rain and erosion to deal with. They were ending the month on a positive note; they were able to get in a decent cutting of hay, get it to the barn, and sell it before any spoilage. Their worst worry of having the crop rest in the field as it dried and then get rained on never materialized.

In the last week of June they decided to take a few days off and go up the river to a favorite fishing spot. There drive was less than a couple of hours away, and they took their twenty-foot boat with its lone Evinrude. Having packed up their fishing gear and a case of beer, they felt ready to catch the big ones. They found a boat launch north of the town of Chelan and just east of Pateros. It was the perfect spot for launching the boat, and after they successfully launched their vessel they were ready to take a chance at the fish. They guided the boat effortlessly up the Columbia, the Evinrude churning a wake behind them. They finally headed toward a promising spot, close enough to the shore but still far enough out that they could get some hits. It was now late enough in the day that the fish would be biting. They came to a stop and then sat quietly, breaking the silence with occasional conversation or the poof of opening a beer. Some time passed, and it was getting on toward the evening. They had caught a few fish between them, and it looked like the hits were slim, so they decided that after another half hour or so they would call it a day. The afternoon and early evening had been ideal; the weather was tolerable, about eighty-two degrees, and only a slight breeze was blowing. The water was calm with exception of the wake the brothers had created with the boat as they trolled along the shore. They were quietly watching their cast-out lines, self-absorbed and feeling the warm afterglow of the beer they had been drinking throughout the afternoon.

Keith began to see his line do an odd dance. He watched intently for several long seconds, and then Jake too began watching as the line rhythmically bounced up and down. The line was not taut but loose, and it danced without anything on the other end. The water that had been so calm throughout the day now began to rise from its sleep. Swells of a couple of feet started to buffet the sides of the boat, although the air was at complete calm with no wind to blame the rolling waters on. Then suddenly, as if to answer the magical dance of the fishing line, the shore and river seemed to do a methodical, oblique dance. The hills beyond tilted, and the river seemed almost detached from the shore. They experienced the upheaval for several seconds until finally the boat was again floating helplessly in waters that were calm once more. Jake and Keith had both fallen back into the boat, and they were still absorbed by the sheer magnitude of the entire phenomenon. They grabbed weakly at the sides of the boat to again sit themselves up. Righting themselves, they began to survey all that was around them. Toward either side of the river they could see a few cars that had pulled off to the side of the road. The people next to their cars were also looking around as if to see whether it was safe to resume their trip. Jake and Keith could see the spillways of Wells Dam; it stood intact. The mountains that had so eerily pitched and yawed for those few seconds now stood silent. The orchards on the sides of the brown hills once again regained their composure. They felt safe but vulnerable on the water, so they hurriedly restarted the Evinrude and aimed the bow toward the loading dock and land.

They loaded the boat onto its trailer and secured it. They checked all the equipment and saw that everything was intact. They felt sure that with all the confusion and the events of the afternoon, they must have lost or misplaced some item or another. They both piled into the pickup as if it were the only thing that could provide them complete safety from the caprices of the world outside their doors. They spoke very little other than to acknowledge that they believed they had been in an earthquake. Neither cared to analyze anything more than that. They drove the pickup along the Columbia. It was again calm, nothing like the angry monster that they both had witnessed and experienced. They took the turnoff up to Chelan Falls, having decided they would stay overnight in one of the cheaper hotels.

They made the trip without further incident, although they had driven extremely slowly, not sure if the road would rise up at them and swallow them up. The first lights of Chelan Falls lit their path, and they found a motel that fit their needs just at the city limits. They parked, went in, rang the bell, and were greeted by a matronly woman. They could see through the open door behind her that she and her family were probably about to sit down for dinner.

As they checked in, Jake and Keith asked the woman if anything unusual had been felt that afternoon in town. Her reply was yes, there had been some commotion and a few odd movements as well as bric-a-brac falling off the shelves. Although it was unheard of, she felt it was not anything cataclysmic.

Jake and Keith left the hotel office and quietly found the room they would be sleeping in. Both were still in a state of post-traumatic stress and were still reeling from their afternoon experience. Jake knew this feeling; he had felt it many years previously while serving in Vietnam. It was something he disliked but was helpless to fight. They managed to park their gear and clean up. They then headed down the road for some dinner and several beers; they needed something to dull their senses if they were going to get any sleep tonight.

They were able to find a small restaurant with a lounge. They ordered dinner and ate in silence, both still too shocked and overwhelmed by the afternoon's activities to bring it up in dinner conversation. They both stared out the window at evening traffic as if to gather up their wits and broach the topic in some manner or fashion, but it didn't happen. They finished their dinners, tipped the waitress, and paid their bill. The lounge was semi-lit, with some good-natured conversation and laughing as patrons ordered their various drinks. The bartender was an older man; portly and good-natured, he busied himself mixing the various concoctions while his single waitress served the thirsty customers. There was a camaraderie, and Jake and Keith soon found themselves involved in conversation with the locals. Some time into the evening, the conversation became a little more loose as the alcohol loosened up their inhibitions. Finally the brothers were talking about their experience on the Columbia with the quake, they learned from the lounge regulars that there had been a few minor aftershocks in the area but nothing of any significance. It was odd, though, as the area had never experienced an earthquake at any time. The brothers had spent a few hours socializing and trying to forget the afternoon; they both were feeling a little heady. Finally they returned to their motel room and immediately fell asleep.

26. Nora

NORA GOT UP, MADE HERSELF coffee, and hurriedly showered and put on her makeup. She was well versed in the morning ritual. Almost as if in a trance, she would shower, apply her makeup, pour herself a cup of coffee, sit down at the table, and smoke a couple of morning cigarettes. She had a cat, but he had been acting odd over the past few days, almost skittish. Later, when she felt the minor aftershocks of the earthquake, she suspected they were the reasons for the cat's behavior. She had heard that the quake was centered above Chelan, and although she wasn't sure of the exact location, she knew the Jake and Keith were somewhere nearby. She hoped and prayed that they would return without incident. No deaths had been reported, and there were only some minor injuries due to sundry items falling from high places. She read that the earthquake was a 5.5 on the Richter scale and felt if ever there was another quake, it would be too soon for her. She spent at least a half hour in her musings and decided it was time to go down to the restaurant.

She would be opening up, and there were several chores to

do in order to get everything up and running and in shipshape. She enjoyed opening; the place was empty and silent in the early morning, and she would see the early morning sun as it peeked through the blinds, as it did every day. She generally started her day by checking the burners and emptying garbage that may have been overlooked. Then she would start the coffee. Not long after her arrival, the cook came in and started his routines. A little after seven, she pulled the blinds, opened the front door, put up the open sign, and greeted the first arrivals as they came through the doors to start their day.

27. A Bout with Nature

Jake and Keith found themselves driving back to Royal City with minimal conversation. They watched the oncoming traffic in muted silence and reflected on their recent encounter with nature with almost a spiritual reverence. In not speaking, they almost felt as if what they had witnessed was a secret they held to themselves, not to be shared with each other and not with anyone else. To relive the event would most assuredly be compromising their sanity; the matter was closed as far as they were concerned.

They arrived home in the late afternoon. Chester met them at the porch when he heard the pickup coming up the driveway, and he watched them as they pulled in, the dust forming tiny clouds behind them as they came closer to the house. They finally stopped the vehicle, and both got out, stretched, and walked toward the house. Chester studied their faces for some indication of what they had encountered on their fishing trip on the upper Columbia. He was aware of the quake and the closeness to the vicinity of where his sons had planned their fishing trip. He felt that they may have had the unfortunate experience of being part of the minor catastrophe. They looked at the old man and said nothing. They walked up to the porch, nodded at him, and went quietly into the house with Chester at their heels. Chester sat down and waited for several minutes. He knew that eventually his sons would speak to him, and he was curious about their silence.

Jack was first to speak. He spoke almost with hesitation, unsure of what the content of his uttering should be, but after several minutes of rambling he was able to get to the point. Chester listened in fascination as his older son revealed how their fishing trip had become a bout with nature. Jack was somewhat reluctant to paint the entire picture, but with Chester's gentle urgings he continued on until the whole story was told. The old man found himself a little envious. In all of his years of living he had never had the experience of encountering the eye of the storm, and he was safe and sound at the house several miles downstream, although he did feel some minor shaking. He finally decided to end his inquisition of his sons; he had heard enough of the event to satisfy his curiosity. He could also see that both his sons were wary of what happened, and there was reluctance to talk about the subject. He felt a little guilty in his cross-examination of them but he knew that his sons would have to talk to him, if not out of respect then out of their subordination to him.

Jake went into town the following morning. He was feeling a little better about talking to Chester, seeing the conversation as a sort of catharsis that let his emotions out. He never could visualize going to a therapist to relive a thousand bad experiences, although his memories of Vietnam still haunted him from time to time, but he felt that this was much different. Nature had risen up against him in a brief and unpredictable manner; there was no words that could adequately describe the whole interlude. He was doing what he felt was the easiest thing, and that was to simply try to forget about the whole incident. His drive into

Royal City was uneventful; it was early morning, and there was not much traffic on the road with exception of an occasional semi. He kept his mind on the road, and when he pulled into town he guided the pickup straight for the restaurant. On his mind were a good hot cup of coffee and Nora, not necessarily in that order.

28. Jake and Nora

Nora was busy serving her first customers of the day. She smiled sweetly at the dusty men in beat-up coveralls and cowboy hats as she scurried about passing plates heaping with eggs and hash browns and at the same time serving coffee with her free hand. She did all this with the dexterity of one who had many years of experience, and her patrons looked upon her graciously. She did not see Jake as he came through the front screen door and did not hear the door as it banged noisily behind him. She first noticed him as some of the other customers acknowledged his entrance and said their hellos as he walked on in and slid into his usual booth. Nora quickly placed the new orders with the cook and checked coffee cups for refilling. Then she went straight to Jake's table. She saw that he looked tired; his smile was empty, and the eyes were not as spirited as she remembered them to be. She sat down across from him and waited for him to say something, anything, in order to break the long and monotonous silence. He did not initiate conversation; that was to be up to Nora. She looked at him carefully. Then slowly, almost in marked cadence, she began to bring him up to date on local gossip that he would not have been privy to in his brief absence. Nora continued on, making some attempt to get Jake to join her in conversation, but she saw that there was reluctance. She finally felt that she was tired of doing all the talking and asked

Jake what had happened on the trip. Did he happen to be in the vicinity of the earthquake, and if he was, what was it like?

Jake thought carefully about what he wanted to say. He looked at Nora and could see that she was genuinely concerned for his well-being, something that Jake was not used to. With hesitation, he relived the whole event for a second time, and for a second time he felt somewhat relieved, as if an enormous weight had been lifted from his shoulders. Nora could see the effect that the episode had on him. She encouraged him to have breakfast and poured some of the hot, black, steamy coffee into his cup,

Jake was grateful for the compassion and the concern that Nora bestowed on him. He sat quietly at the table as the patrons who had finished paid their bills and left, only to be replaced by more patrons coming in for their breakfast. Jake ate resolutely, almost stoically, chewing on the ham and eggs and sipping his coffee while thinking about the past week over and over. He finished, and Nora brought over another refill of coffee, no bill; the breakfast was on her. He made adjustments, straightening his hat, and winked at Nora as he began to walk out the door. She caught him just before his exit. She hugged him, smiling warmly, and whispered in his ear that she would see him later, maybe that evening if he wasn't too busy, Jake nodded, kissed her lightly on the cheek, and walked through the door out into the sunlight.

29. Discovery

KIRK AND HIS STUDENTS SPENT their first days setting up. Kirk had a gung-ho, take-no-prisoners attitude and wanted to proceed on that path. His whole life was science, and at the pinnacle of that, geology reigns supreme. He looked about the camp. Here and there were the various advances of technology:

satellite dishes, laptops, cell phones, and various other gadgets that would be used to analyze and send via e-mail the discoveries that were bound to follow in the proceeding days of their search. Kirk's colleagues were all capable and knowledgeable; a few were PhDs, and several were graduate students, all respected in the field. Kirk set about checking the campsite they had decided on: a spot near Lake Roosevelt, easy enough to get to by four-wheel drive and fairly close to the site of the initial discovery. The campsite was well provisioned; they had more than enough supplies of canned goods and water to last them a month, despite estimating that they would not need any longer than a couple of weeks to do their surveying and information gathering. For the sake of their mentor and their sanity, they brought the extra commodities all on Kirk's persistent ramblings. As the evening crept upon them, they all watched as the sun took its last peek over the horizon and set slowly in the west.

There was a redness in the sky. A couple of the students mumbled to themselves the old sailor's adage of "Red sky at night, sailor's delight," and felt that this would be an omen. Kirk looked about their base camp, satisfied with the results of hard work and organization. Everything was in place for the days to come. Now as darkness began to enshroud the camp, fires were started. Tiny sparks drifted heavenward as the crackling and popping of twigs and wood punctuated the air around them. They started their dinners. Some were creative, mixing chili with fried potatoes and onions, eating their fill only to suffer with heartburn later in the night. These victuals were washed down by cold beer and plenty of good-natured gossip to loosen the spirit.

In the morning, men started stirring in their sleeping bags with the rising sun. Already, Kirk and a few of the others were busily stirring the embers of smoldering fire with the hopes of restarting it. They piled on just enough flammable material so the fire could find its life once again. They had success: the fire caught its breath. The materials were dry enough, and the oxygen was right. With the fire started, they put a large pot of coffee on the rocks that surrounded it. Then they cracked eggs and laid bacon into cast-iron skillets and placed these within the confines of the flames. The bacon and eggs began to cook, splattering and popping, as the odor of coffee wafted through the campsite, finally waking the others with its pungent and tempting odor. Slowly the remainder of the men sleepily came out of their tents, all rubbing their eyes vigorously, clearing away the last vestiges of sleep and glimpsing the beginnings of a new day. They set about washing themselves, brushing their teeth, and relieving themselves. With their morning toilet behind them, they soon sat down to their breakfast and the hot, steaming coffee. Within the hour, their day would begin.

They all finished breakfast by a little after six. Their plates were devoid of leftovers: all had eaten heartily, and it would be several hours before another meal. The men cleaned up after themselves, picking up any of the remnants that had spilled and stowing away any items that would be of interest to the local varmints, coyotes in particular. They spoke little in the early-morning air, focusing only on what they would need for the upcoming hours. They rummaged through their tents, picked up items they thought would be necessary for their trek, and then put on hiking boots. They were ready to embark on the beginning of their destiny.

Kirk, too, wasted no time in getting his equipment at the ready. He looked around his campsite and located a map that would come in handy for the days to come. He also would bring along the cell phone with the all-important satellite link; civilization was just a call away if that crucial find surfaced. He stepped back out into the morning air. They were all prepared for a hot day; it was well into summer, and shade was a luxury that would not be afforded to them. They were in sagebrush country, barren and primitive with exception of Lake Roosevelt and Banks Lake in the vicinity. Kirk looked over the camp, saw that everything was stowed away, and then took a long glance at his team, almost like a general reviewing his troops before the final crucial battle. With a grunt of satisfaction, he nodded his confirmation to them that they would start.

In the hill country along the lake, the men trudged along. They navigated over the ancient remnants of volcanic rock and the escarpments created by millions of years of natural creativity, the movement of glaciers that reworked the terrain into an austere and almost cosmic form. They followed a path that had allowed others to pass, here and there, along the rocky inclines. Often someone would stumble on the loose and jagged rocks.

They circumnavigated around one of the tall cliffs, a plateau at its summit. They had decided that instead of returning to the initial site of discovery, they would ascend to a greater height for a far better view. They continued on, gradually beginning their ascent. All were in fairly good physical condition, but the climb was still challenging, and all carried backpacks with thirty to forty pounds of necessities. The climb became more vertical to the point of moving hand over hand. Without gear to belay with, they found themselves struggling for every foothold, but there were ledges and cracks enough to gain an advantage over their climb upward. They spent the morning and much of the afternoon climbing until they finally gained the top of the plateau and their first unobstructed view of the topography below. They all let out a sigh of relief upon reaching their destination. Each man slowly and methodically took off the burden that he had carried on his back for the last several hours. Sweat soaked their clothing, and all felt the unquenchable thirst that comes with a maximum of physical exertion. With the packs resting on the ground, the men sat down heavily and drank with gusto from their canteens.

The top was flat and dotted here and there with the crabgrass and weed-like growth often found in barren, austere landscapes. They were, after all, in what was and still is the sagebrush country of Eastern Washington. They looked over what would be their first work station. The plateau was a good half a mile in circumference, more than enough to set up a camp and their equipment. There was a decent drop-off of perhaps a couple hundred feet that met the gentle sloping of the foothills below. Beyond that were other plateaus that ringed about the landscape and the lakes off in the distance. A few miles to their east, they saw a partially obstructed view of the spillways of Grand Coulee. They took in the magnificence of the panorama's beauty and grace as well as its rawness with the awe of weary travelers seeing a cut of nature's best for the first time.

 Kirk moved slowly to the edge of the cliff and looked down. He had difficulty comprehending the physical task each man had undertaken in making his ascent to where they now spoke freely. The men walked about cajoling one another as well as congratulating each other on their climb. Kirk brought out a high-powered pair of Bausch and Lomb binoculars and began to slowly scan the geography; he made a sweeping gesture from north to south and then east to west, moving his gaze in layers so as to not miss a landmark that might reveal something of value. He spent the next hour or so in this effort, making mental notes of disparities and where they were located. He later decided to forego this exercise and set up some of the more sophisticated hardware that the team had brought along. He started barking orders to his subordinates about what they would need to assemble and began to eye the deep plateaus and the cliffs with his unobstructed eye. In Kirk's initial sighting, he saw what had appeared to be a rift, a gentle, sloping line that ran laterally along the cliffs on the opposing side of the lake. He was unable to ascertain its point of beginning, but it appeared to run from west to east and proceed under the water's surface. It was much longer and wider than their initial discovery. Kirk was eager to get a better view of this latest find.

The men started setting up the scopes, tripods, laser-guided systems, and even a satellite dish. They would be staying here overnight, hundreds of feet up from the basin floor, guided by one man in his quest to redefine the earth and its natural state. They knew he was on to something; they themselves were able to visualize the deep furrow on the opposite side of the canyons. They were also a little apprehensive of the ramifications of the new find. There was haste in their work to set up all the technological equipment that would help in gaining the knowledge that they thirsted for. They proceeded smoothly; each man knew what was required of him and went about the task silently, almost stealthily. Several tripods with scopes were now facing the opposite side of the canyon walls and lake below. The men began to look through the lenses, stopping only to write down the coordinates on scraps of paper they had carried with them. Kirk used a surveyor's transom to gain perspective of distance and stopped only briefly to concur with colleagues on his findings and theirs.

The day was long and hot; they had often drenched themselves from their canteens to cool off, but they continued their work up until the evening, stopping only to watch a spectacular setting sun as it dropped out of sight in the west. The day had proven to be rewarding. As the men sat around that night, they were able to see what they had accomplished. The Earth had moved; their notes would illustrate this. They now needed more. They would have to go to the other side and explore the site.

30. Inner Bowels

Inside Grand Coulee, technicians and engineers alike spent several days checking and rechecking all the systems that made the giant behemoth tick. Structurally the dam was no Titanic; she was built to last, and those who labored inside her bowels knew of her strength. There were minor concerns, though. The quake was several miles downstream, and although minor it could have an effect on the operating of the dam, causing anomalies in instruments and problems with transferring on and off the power grids. Lastly, it could lead to the formation of minute cracks. So the dam was checked inside and out. The power houses that housed the thirty-two Westinghouse turbines showed no damage, no telltale signs of cracking or injury that could be a major problem later on. Outside, the face was inspected with no disregard for the minute, for it was the obscure that could bring even this Goliath to its knees. Having found the dam intact and its integrity sound, the workers felt resolute. Life continued on without delay. Some days later, after the inspection had revealed no difficulties, a technician noted an artifact in one of the many gauges that he stared at nightly. It was of minimal concern—gauges had acted up before—but there was a sequence that alarmed him. He reported it to a night supervisor and then put the problem out of his mind.

31. A Trip to Nora's

Jake finished up with the dinner plates. The Henderson men often took turns in cleaning up after dinner. Now with Chester's handicap, the chore fell to Jake and Keith. Dinner was always a mundane affair; often it was nothing more than a microwave meal or bacon and eggs. Tonight it was leftover roast from two days past, still edible. When Jake finished up, the old man was already snoring in his overstuffed lazy boy. He went outside. Keith was already sitting on the porch, smoke curling away from him as he stared out into space. Jake sat down and lit his cigarette. He stared thoughtfully at the match before snuffing it out and then inhaled deeply. The evening was calm and warm; the men looked out over their fields and said nothing, quietly reflecting on the day's activities and accomplishments.

Keith took a final draw on his cigarette, exhaled the unwanted smoke, and put it in an ashtray already overfilled with butts. He looked over toward Jake and spoke. He, too, had carried the stressors of the recent earthquake and needed to talk about the incident. He looked to Jake as a willing participant. Keith had avoided Chester's prying questions on the subject with great finesse, but he still needed to vocalize how he felt. He spoke almost haltingly; the episode was indelibly etched in his consciousness, and he needed the support of his brother. At times he felt that his sanity had been tested, but as he continued recounting the event to Jake, he started to feel the same uplifting that Jake had experienced. Their conversation lasted several minutes. Jake nodding now and then, speaking up only when Keith would question him on his own feelings. He finally concluded his train of thought, and Jake gave him the support that was expected of him. He told Keith that they had survived and left it at that. Jake got up out of his chair, said he was going to town, and left.

As Jake walked across the yard, the evening sky was approaching. It was bright red and glorious, a beautiful July night, and it was only eight o'clock. Off in the fields he heard the killdeer as it made its shrill calls. The smell of new hay accosted his nose. He enjoyed this time of the year. In the truck, he turned over the engine, backed up, then finally shifted into first and headed out onto the highway, guiding himself toward town and Nora. He drove in silence. He had thought that Keith would attempt to hitch a ride with him and was happy that he stayed back at the house. He told no one of his date with Nora, not feeling that it was anyone's business. He didn't often go to town in the evening, and this night in particular was a solo run. He did feel that his role as therapist to Keith had been helpful, not only to Keith but to himself as well. It was the only action that would eventually salve the festering wound and provide a modicum of relief, facilitating a return to normalcy in their lives.

Jake kept on driving and started up the final incline and straightaway before the highway wound into Royal City. His thoughts now were entirely on Nora and had been over the past few miles, uninterrupted by anything else. It was as if the closer he got to her, the more urgent his need to see her became. Jake had spent evenings with Nora before; their relationship, though, was in its infancy. They were slowly getting to know one another's likes and dislikes. Each had a tale of woe, old baggage, and past relationships that still haunted them. They were essentially relearning how to care for someone else. So with that Jake pulled into town, wheeled into a parking place outside the apartment building where Nora lived, and smiled smugly to himself.

This evening was not different from others, but in some odd way Jake's encounter with nature and Nora's need to nurture him had caused their feelings for each other to intensify. Their compassion increased their passion for one another. This had become evident that morning when Nora had made her overture to Jake to meet that evening.

Jake felt a shiver of excitement. He climbed the stairs to her apartment briskly, often striding two at a time, and was on the landing before he realized his progress. He knocked gently on the open door. He could see the dimly lit room through the screen; the night was warm, and Nora had chosen to leave the door open, Nora soon appeared at the door, smiling warmly. She had let her hair down, and soft rivulets ringed her face.

She had on only a hint of makeup and lipstick to accentuate her features. She dressed simply in, a white blouse and a denim dress. The outcome made Jake breathless. She looked younger and much more beautiful than he had ever seen her before. Nora felt Jake's eyes upon her. Then she finally met his gaze with her eyes. She spoke softly, reaching out for him. She brought him into the apartment, and they sat on the sofa. There the mastery of her femaleness brought Jake into her orbit. They had planned to go out to a nearby restaurant, but the plan failed. The throes of lust found them holding each other tightly, hotly, and finally without clothing, wreathing, sweating, and undulating in a night that was filled with their need for each other. Later, hours after they had again consummated their passion, they sought out the refuge of each other's warmth. Nora placed her head in the crook of Jake's neck, gently rubbing the hair on his chest, and eventually surrendered to sleep and contentment.

The two lovers slept soundly, uninhibited. They slept the sleep that only lovers can share, restful and peaceful. Morning came. Upon awaking they again became entwined and one, holding each other with exhilaration and gentleness. They were now together.

They awoke simultaneously, nuzzling one another and making the promises lovers make after a night of lovemaking. They had no time to renew the fervor; morning was coming on, and the day needed to begin, regardless of their new commitment to one another. They got out of their bed, kissed and hugged each other, and then briskly got dressed and went their individual ways.

32. The Miniature Sub

In the Pacific, a scientific research boat had been sent out to measure disturbance in the offshore plates so renowned for their underwater activities. This research effort was motivated by the recent developments that Kirk and his colleagues had been investigating on land. The craft was well off the coast, a good sixty to seventy miles. Its sole duty was to report any new activity in the tectonic plates. They operated with a miniature sub that would investigate depths up to eight miles below surface. The depth was challenging given the forces of nature. The outside pressures were so great that the craft itself underwent some changes in its configuration. Nevertheless, scientists on board took the careful readings required of them as well as viewing the natural caldron of the earth's crusts seething as it poured forth with long fingers, exploring the oceans floor. The two men on board the sub would spend hours in their search, noting the new exceptions to an already fragile environment. The frontier they explored had been charted before. Numerous forms of life, colorful and flagellating in direct contradiction to the boundaries of life, lived at these depths, surviving the most momentous of challenging habitats. In the same visual field, their eyes saw the foaming of white to red molten rock, a miniature volcano in the making and being born before their eyes. This was a new development. The great plates that brought continents together were doing their primeval grind, answering to nature's directions. The men, always in direct communication to the command ship, immediately reported the findings.

Topside, the research vessel that accompanied the sub to its destination floated lazily in the calm waters. The crew had all been busy throughout the morning starting with the sub launching. That process had not only required the rigors of battening the vessel down but also the detailed checking and rechecking of her integrity before she could submerge. Sundry crew members now gathered in the command center of the ship. The captain left the wheel to his first mate and joined the various scientists, oceanographers, and others as information from the sub flashed on their screens. They saw the telegraphed visions of a gaping inferno, apocalyptic and absorbing. The audience watched as lava spewed onto the ocean floor, a long separation seeking the route of least resistance, opening the ocean floor and revealing its angry spirit. They watched incredulously as the event occurred. No one talked for several moments; the more experienced of the scientists who had been in these locales before waited for comments from colleagues. Finally a sole voice said, "We have a—"

33. Paranoia

CHRIS HAD SPENT THE BEGINNING of his summer in a spirit of paranoia. He had destroyed software that could incriminate him in the chaos he brought upon the BPA. He knew, however, that their investigation would continue until they had apprehended the culprit and had prosecuted him or her. Yet strangely, this knowledge didn't affect him. Chris couldn't see the oddness of his behavior. He attributed it all to the recent events and the suspicion that he was always being followed. He started to isolate himself from his friends and family, finding his room to be a safe haven from the outside world. The friends with whom he had spent so much time during the school year were now considered as suspect with their own set of motives. They soon gave up on Chris as he slipped further and further into his own world.

Chris initially started a summer job in a local McDonalds. He was working the afternoon shift until early July, when his sanity took a turn for the worse. He had been bickering back and forth with an assistant manager who he suspected had it in for him. His thinking was not far from the truth: the manager disliked him immensely, but delusional thoughts were becoming more pervasive in Chris's psyche daily. Chris, increasingly out of touch with reality, grabbed a fistful of hamburgers that were still under the warming lights and flung them haphazardly into a stunned audience of customers waiting to place their orders. Before staff could subdue him, he was able to fling French fries, soft drinks, and sundry other foodstuffs into the retreating crowds. His finale was to remove several twenty-dollar bills with a few tens and vault the countertop, seeking the anonymity of the street.

Chris ran several blocks. The car in which he had driven to work was still at the drive-in. His mind was churning and disorganized, but in the nature of his work no one had noticed the subtleties of his behaviors. He kept to himself and seldom sought the advice of others. Everyone had their own bouts of incapacitation, and inquiry was not a priority. With his wild escape and the madness of the event, Chris felt exuberant. His robbery was justified in his mind: he had worked several hours and felt entitled to the cash. He spent the rest of the afternoon in and out of alleys and assorted other hiding places, dodging police and an assortment of McDonald's employees, who were seeking their own brand of justice and vigilantism.

Chris slowly wound his way back to the security of his parents' house. He could not and did not know that the police had been there several times throughout the day, hoping to catch him there. He spent several minutes in the camouflage of several bushes that ran the perimeter of the home waiting for falling darkness and a chance to sneak into the house unobserved. Unmarked police cars waited for him.

Chris found his way into the King County mental health system involuntarily. His parents had long suspected that his recent aberrant behaviors were an exit from his routine zany self. They felt at odds with his seclusion and loss of interest in friends, so they watched him carefully. Chris had destroyed the software that could have incriminated him to the BPA prior to his break, so he was not suspected in that. The police had no suspicions about his recent past of hacking. He was initially taken to the local precinct, where he was booked and fingerprinted. Police had interviewed his parents before Chris's apprehension, and they had explained their suspicions that he needed psychiatric care. The police were more than happy to oblige; they already had a severe backup in the dockets for hearings. Soon after his brief encounter with the police, Chris was rushed off top Harborview for a psychiatric evaluation and his introduction into the King County mental health system.

The manager at the McDonald's did not press charges in light of Chris's state of mind and the apprehension; all he asked for was the return of the money Chris had taken. He sympathized with his ex-employee's parents, but in the back of his mind he was glad about the turn of events. He had never felt comfortable with Chris, and even though he was hard pressed to find anything lacking in the young man's competency, he didn't trust Chris's solitary nature and his reluctance to join in on the restaurant camaraderie during business lulls. Everything had worked out for the better.

On a warm June night, Chris was rushed to Harborview. The police took him in their cruiser with parents following behind. Chris looked absently out the rear window of the police car, his hands handcuffed for fear of possible escape, though the thought had not even entered his mind. They parked outside the emergency entrance and escorted Chris into the hospital. Nurses on duty in triage wasted no effort in determining the nature of Chris's problem. They could see that there was some need to make haste after seeing the police with their handcuffed fugitive. They quickly directed Chris and his parents back to assessment and placed them in a private room so one of the on-call psychiatrists could evaluate the patient and make a determination on his sanity. Outside the exam room, nurses and doctors rushed around in controlled chaos. Already the Friday evening was becoming more and more frantic as the city began to come alive. Sirens often wailed, and the hallways of the emergency section were being filled with gurneys holding the various victims of trauma, alcohol, and a wide assortment of other injuries.

Chris seemed oblivious to all the mayhem that was around him. The door to the exam room that he occupied was ajar, and he missed little of the excitement in the hallways outside. Chris absorbed the scene with contentment. He was incapable, though, of fully understanding his current predicament. He looked at his parents' worried faces to seek some sort of absolution or understanding of what was happening to him now.

A man finally rapped on the door. After receiving approval to enter, he walked in and quietly observed everyone in the room. He had already looked at Chris's chart and in his conscience had also made his ruling. It was now up to the principal players to provide him with their testimony in regard to Chris's recent twist of behavior. The police were familiar with the tall, dignified psychiatrist; they had brought others to his domain for evaluation. Many had entered the clandestine world of involuntary commitment. The doctor, having absorbed the energies of the room, introduced himself. Without hesitation, he asked his questions randomly, first of the parents, then of Chris, and then, briefly, of the police officers who had accommodated Chris to the exam. He delved into all of Chris's past behaviors and saw where the break had occurred. Then, with a nod, he took the parents into another room and questioned them further. With the relief of not having to talk in front of their only child, they felt secure. Being in the sanctum with the doctor's calm and reassuring voice encouraged them to open up and relay all the events that had brought them to this day. They did not deny that the evidence was overwhelming. Dr. Hummel acknowledged the great misfortune that they were currently involved in. Looking with sincerity upon this family, he said the commitment would stand. Chris would enter a local mental hospital after the commitment papers were signed because he was a danger to himself or others.

Doctor and family reentered the exam room. Chris was staring off into space; his mood was sour. He felt that he was not in control of whatever was occurring in his life and that decisions were being made without his contribution. He looked up at the doctor and then at his parents, searching their faces for answers. They looked at him blankly, almost with guilt. Chris knew this was a portent of his future. He waited apprehensively for the silence to be broken. Dr. Hummel sat down, as did Chris's parents. The police had been urged to step out of the room by the good doctor.

The key players were now in place, and the doctor began his soliloquy. He guided Chris through the events of the day and the recent past, here and there with acknowledgment from his parents to prop his arguments of Chris's insanity. Chris was bemused as the litany of his acts became more of a fascination than a concern. He couldn't understand what the big deal was about. The doctor was professional; he laid out the evidence with uncanny accuracy and then waited for his patient to reply or rebel. Chris sat quietly, bent his head down, and wept. He was beginning to understand the gravity of all that had occurred. The doctor delivered his dictum and then left the room to sign the various legal forms. The parents would be the petitioners. Chris was helpless for the first time in his life.

34. Fissures

Kirk and his companions spent several days on the plateau. Far down below them was the outstretched lake behind Grand Coulee Dam. The deep canyons and jutting rocks gave way to the makeup of the harsh environment. They spent time between the two encampments, but Kirk himself had decided upon the plateau. Over the span of several days they were able to see what had appeared as a rift, which proceeded along in a horizontal line for several hundred yards. They noted the coordinates. Their measurements showed that it was stationary; its length was exact and without change. The researchers mapped the location and compared their results to satellite photos that Kirk printed. They would eventually move to the opposite side of their location, but they still needed more diagnostics before the move. They were involved with observation at this point; the physical investigation would take place when they moved.

As luck would have it, nature took the first step. Kirk spent the afternoon downloading information sent to him from the lab in Seattle. In the material was a quick reference to what was believed to be rifting and volcanic activity in the Pacific. Kirk read the material with keen interest. The coordinates of the offshore quaking were in direct line with where they were carrying on their studies. As for the time, it was within hours of Kirk actually downloading the material. The morning had not been spent observing the geologic character of the cliffs opposite their camp; rather, it was a slow day. Men had gathered up their belongings and begun to make ready for their exit from one plain to go to another. Kirk halted their efforts with immediacy. He had them set up their various telescopes and other technological aids to get one more glance at their rift before they broke camp.

Kirk was the first to view the rift, several meters distant but unhampered by any obscurity. Kirk saw that what previously had been several hundred yards in length had increased in its length by several hundred more yards. It ran perilously close to the lake and at one point appeared to enter the lake, playing a sort of geologic game of tag with the cliffs above and the water below, Kirk slowly moved away from the scope and then urged his team to each investigate the development. Each man took a turn looking through the scope toward the rift beyond. All spent several minutes looking at the fissure with great curiosity and awe. After they had looked at the new find and had satisfied their own desire to see this new twist in geologic architecture, they moved away and nodded to their colleagues to take their turn. After they had finished, Kirk made a few notes and spoke to the men to see that they were all in agreement with the physical find. Consensus being met, they began their trek down.

The men spent much of the day going down the steep cliff that they had climbed up days ago. The trip down was much more harrowing in nature: several of them slipped, and there were many cuts and abrasions from the shale and loose rock. The descent was tedious and dangerous; the equipment each man carried made him a walking pack horse. Stops were frequent as packs were readjusted and secured. The sun also had become their enemy. While on top of the plateau, they had the luxury of shade. By the use of canvas tarpaulins, they were not fully exposed. The daytime temperature was now in the upper nineties. The snakes were also out. Here and there was a sunning rattler. They let those who came too close know their locale with their cautioning tails. Nobody was bitten, but there were a few close calls.

Kirk's team kept up their momentum, winding slowly down the rough trail that they had broken only days previously. There was an enthusiastic spirit amongst them; all were consumed in getting to the bottom and going over to the site of their find in order to get a closer look at the rift and take all the necessary measurements and observations. After several hours of their rugged descent to the bottom, they finally reached their destination. Each man sat down, heavily took off his burdensome backpack, and then took a long drink of water from his canteen. The water was warm, but that did not hinder their thirst. They rested for several minutes, lazily squinting up at the high cliffs that surrounded them and primarily at the site that they had left earlier that morning. They all felt a sense of invincibility from being able to conquer the cliff without serious injury or snakebite. Kirk, seeing that his team looked adequately refreshed, urged them to get up and make the brief trip back to their vehicles.

The men trekked back to their four-wheel vehicles and packed the equipment on board. They would have liked the opportunity of going into town, renting a nice clean room, bathing, eating a steak, and then sleeping through the night on a firm mattress, but this was not meant to be. Kirk, being the taskmaster he was, encouraged each and every one of his team members to rise to the occasion and never to utter a negative comment. It worked; the men were all as focused as Kirk himself. They started their vehicles and proceeded in single file. They were approaching a primitive road, so their progress was slow until they hit the highway. They followed behind each other and finally crossed over the river in parade-like fashion, all absorbed in what they would encounter once they had exited the highway and found a trail that would lead them back to their rift. They continued down the highway for several miles until Kirk, who was in the lead vehicle, pulled off the highway to see if they were in the approximate area opposite the plateau. He got out of his truck and stood with binoculars, staring off toward the cliffs on the opposite side of the canyons. He was able to pick out some of the more observable characteristics of the cliffs that would identify where they had been. He satisfied himself with what he had seen and then, with the others following behind, walked several hundred feet on the sandy, rocky soil to see if they could pick up a trail to their new destination.

Kirk was able to spot part of the fissure. It was still fresh in his memory from his previous visit in the spring, and he saw where they could at least drive part of the way, thus saving them time as well as the effort of carrying the equipment manually to the site. They all returned to their vehicles after a briefing from Kirk on how to avoid some of the pitfalls of navigating down steep inclines and loose rock. They listened intently; many of them were having their first encounters with the hazardous driving that they were now experiencing, and they welcomed Kirk's advice. They all returned to their trucks and one by one followed Kirk down a steep incline at low gear. They managed to avoid the deep ruts and erosion brought on by previous spring rains and eventually found a primitive pullout that was big enough to park all the vehicles without too much difficulty. They had all arrived intact. Driving out would be slightly easier, provided they did not encounter anybody coming down the opposite direction.

They parked and set the emergency brakes in order to avoid the loss of any of their rolling stock. The cliffs were almost vertical in some areas, so caution was used in every regard. Kirk checked one of his many maps and briefly spoke with one of the more senior members of the crew. Then he turned his attentions to Paul, the student who had made the initial find. He quizzed the young student's about what he would be looking for when they finally returned to the site. Paul was thoughtful with his answer; he considered their priorities in reinvestigating the fissure without destroying any of the evidence. After some time had passed, he gave a brief reply stating his position. Kirk was satisfied with his student's reply.

They were all eager to begin their trek down to the site of their initial find. Kirk sensed their exuberance and glee. He, too, had felt the same way as the young grad students, but he would not let the spirit of the moment blind their objectivity. This was first and foremost a scientific survey, and it would rely on perfection when the actual data gathering proceeded. They began to look about for the best access to their site of interest. One of the younger students spotted a small trail approximately twenty five yards from where they had parked their vehicles. It would be a steep descent, but most of their day had involved mountain climbing, and they still had enough light to make some progress. Kirk looked out to the west to judge the remaining light and decided that they could get to the site with enough time to actually pursue some of their physical gathering of data. He let the setting sun set the pace as the canyons around them began to soak up the rays of last light and shadows began to lengthen. The men made haste to begin the climb down to the rudimentary trail below them, all cautiously watching for the loose rock that could mean a slip, slide, or tumble off the side of the cliff and into the afterlife. The climb down to the trail went smoothly. After they had reached their goal, they all readjusted backpacks and canteens and began their slow procession in single file to the beginning of the fissure.

They got their first glimpse of the abyss at around seven o'clock. It had opened up its mouth and appeared to sneer at the young men who had come to examine it. They all set down their equipment and walked up to what was the beginning of a small cave which went far underground. No one ventured into it; there were too many hazards associated with spelunking into unknown openings. The cave was not the initial find from earlier in the Spring; they were more interested in the long furrow that they had seen from so many meters away. They decided with the waning sunlight that the project would have to wait until the following morning. With that, they busily pitched their tents and made a rudimentary campsite to accommodate their needs for that evening. They all ate a small meal of jerky and other sundry items. Then they spent a brief time talking about the progress they had made and what they would be accomplishing the following morning. By nine o'clock, the sun had set, and the men were in the throes of their dreams, sleeping soundly.

35. The Jigsaw

Kirk was the first of the men to wake. His night was fitful; he tossed and turned throughout the night thinking about the following day and the significance of what they would be looking at. The morning arrived early for him, and although he had not slept, his body was full of energy. Kirk quietly arose from his sleeping bag and then rolled it up, all this without unwanted disturbance to save the others who still slept a few extra moments of needed rest before the day's demands. He came out of his tent and was greeted by the slow beginnings of daylight as the sun began its rise in the east. He looked at the cliffs that surrounded him, and off to the west he could see the beginnings of light on the rocky precipices as the rays of sun started to bathe the rocky spires in the morning requiem. The sight was accommodated by the beginning warmth that would surely provide another hot day and monotonous hours in an unrelenting sun. Now others began to move restlessly. The dawn was peeking into their tents, nature tugging at their sleep and encouraging them to wake. Kirk looked again heavenward. High overhead was a hawk, soaring effortlessly in the beginning currents of heat that rose from the canyon floors. He watched the magnificent bird's parabolas, admiring its physical ability and its determination. After several minutes, he returned his attentions to the waking camp.

They were all awake now. The sun was up and providing the day's first light. The team began to roll up sleeping bags, collect materials that would be needed for the demands of the day, and, most important, gather up some of the chaparral that could be used as a base for a campfire and breakfast. Their first hour after waking was busy; all looked at the day with anticipation. They ate a breakfast of bacon and biscuits that softened nicely with the morning coffee, ate ravenously, and made conversation in between bites. After finishing, they cleaned up the eating utensils, doused the fire to extinction, and were ready for the beginning of the day.

Kirk and Paul had reviewed their previous findings while the other men had been eating their breakfast. Paul was selected for the obvious reason that he had been the discoverer of the rift, and it was necessary to debrief him for his memory of the site they would be returning to. Part of the day would be spent taking accurate measurements of the cave-like appendage. Then they would move along in an easterly direction, following the direct line of the fissure. After Kirk and Paul had reviewed some of the maps from their previous trip, complete with the actual coordinates and accuracy being provided by satellite, they then turned their attentions to the recent findings by the oceanographic researchers, who had alerted them to the movement offshore. All this evidence was beginning to shape up as several pieces of an uncompleted jigsaw puzzle. They both reviewed all the information with some element of pessimism.

Kirk and Paul finished their consultation and talked over their concerns and findings with the more senior members of the group. They found areas of agreement as well as discord amongst themselves and decided that accurate answers would be provided only by the day's exploration. They all gathered up backpacks and began the day's work. Starting at the cave, a couple of them began the work of taking measurements of depth and width as well as noting any changes of the physical geology of the site since spring, The rest moved on, walking along the crags, crabgrass, and rocky terrain. They picked through the vegetation and closely analyzed the sites that needed definition and measurement. The team spent the entire morning and well into the afternoon involved in their cataloging efforts, all attention focused on being precise and not missing any of the minutiae that could result in error.

As day approached the noon hours and the sun rose higher, the men stripped down, wrapped T-shirts around their heads in makeshift sweatbands, and continued on with the tedious but rewarding work. They had decided that with the encroaching day, the gathering of all the measurements would be too time-consuming, so instead they chose to follow the long, unbroken line that seemed to glide effortlessly through the rocky sediment, leaving its calling card in details etched like giant cracks in an egg. The fissure was jagged at places, choosing to take the path of least resistance in some of the harder rock. Much of what they were looking at was the remains of past volcanic action, the sediment left over from millions of years and found in much of the basin area and the eastern part of the state. Although they had decided that the mapping would be done over several days, they did gather the rudimentary data they would need at the end of the day. Kirk stopped briefly every hour or so to feed the information into the laptop that he was becoming more and more dependent on, later it would be downloaded and the details analyzed. They continued, at times stopping here and there and taking special note of specific areas that seemed to defy the written laws of geology: huge rocks displaced where the movement of nature threw them aside like so much flotsam, placing them below the site of the rift and then moving on in its progression to gain a foothold farther east, inching by feet, then yards, and finally miles.

Kirk and his team grew more and more astonished at the strength of the geologic advance. They came across their earlier site of discovery early in the day, looked carefully at it, and made their observations of how the extension joined to it. They moved on for several miles, until they were following the abyss into the shallows of Lake Roosevelt. The trail stopped at the shoreline. The men were baffled on how to proceed; there was no way they could follow the unbroken line any farther, so they sat down and pondered the next step. Kirk looked gravely at the lines of egress from its rocky inclines into the smooth, blue waters of the lake. He felt as though their find had somehow managed to escape their grasp. He took a second long look at the course that he imagined the fissure would take. His eyes led him to a slight bend in the lake, where he could see the beginnings of several large spillways of the Grand Coulee Dam and the sloping hills on either side. He said nothing to his team, who watched him as he put his input into the laptop, taking careful calculations of the findings. Then without hesitation, each man got back to his feet and began following Kirk as he began walking back to their point of departure.

They walked back to their campsite in half the time it had taken them to cover the several miles down to the lake. They were all worn out, and all of them knew that what they had discovered was extremely important. They would spend the next several days carefully redefining the existing maps of their locale with the added demarcation of an unending rift running its geologic finger along the base of cliffs and beyond, separating old from old and doing so with ominous undertones. Kirk decided with consensus from his team that the Army Corps Of Engineers would have to be made privy to their findings, for all the obvious reasons. But in the meantime, they would go over every inch of the fault with all the technological expertise that was at their disposal.

36. Billy Red Bones

Billy Red Bones returned to his old ways, back to the alcohol that fueled past anger and uncertainty. He had spent several days locked in the gloom of not knowing what would become of the future. Billy had never actually been one for deep philosophical thought, but as his years advanced and the uncertainty around him became more realistic, he found himself in despair. After the incarceration in Moses Lake, he had put great effort into maintaining sobriety. He had lost his car in that adventure; unable to pay the towing charge and storage fees, he had left the vehicle to nature and rust. With his loss of transportation he lost some of his independence, and hated having to rely on others to do various errands. One of his old friends, a Yakama by the name of Red Hawk, had been dropping by on a regular basis. After Billy's release from the Grant County jail, his friend decided to talk him into going to AA. Billy had never been receptive to AA; he felt that his battles with the drink were survivable, so he put the idea to the back of his mind until the urgings of his friend. He finally decided that there was nothing to lose, for the next several weeks Billy and Red Owl made the trip into an AA clubhouse once or twice a week. Billy seemed to be absorbing the camaraderie of the members of the AA meetings that they were attending, but after a couple of months of hearing and rehearing some of the old war stories of the reformed drunks, Billy grew restless again. He quit going. His friend came around, but Billy was quick with excuses as to why he couldn't go to the meetings. Red Owl finally got the clue and avoided coming to pick up Billy.

In his heart Billy was saddened. He looked around at what had been his shelter since he had been a young man. The ramshackle trailer with the plywood tarpaper addition had been a hand-me-down, a piece of land willed to him after his father's death at an early age from alcoholism. Billy had never known his mother. In the full spectrum of life's folly, Billy had been handed all manner of bad luck and melancholy. Billy also had an older brother who had managed to get himself killed some years back in a fight on the Yakama reservation over a card game fueled by cheap beer. Billy's life had been full of tragedy. Now, well into his fortieth year, the turnarounds were sluggish. His only support was a disability check that came in once a month for an old construction injury that left him with a game leg and bad balance. He often used a walking stick to get around, and with the drinking, locomotion was often an adventure. Some years back he had been flush with some old tribal monies. The small piece of land that he now lived on was to be renovated with the tribal funds, but it never happened. Billy was not one to pass on opportunities; like the few others left in his tribe, he had spent the money foolishly, often in week-long parties and extravagances that he could ill afford.

Billy's only redeeming possession was the few acres of desolate land that he lived on close to the Columbia. He held on to it, not out of future speculation but as a place to dream of the old ways of the river and the gill netting that he as a young child had enjoyed so much along, with the rest of his family and tribal elders. The memories that lingered in his mind were all gone now, so with nothing invested he lived meagerly, from monthly check to monthly check. This income was often spent in a matter of days; then he struggled for the rest of the month to make ends meet. The ironic part of this existence was the speculation that was moving closer and closer toward his plot of ground. It moved from the west, Seattle. As the oversaturated coast sought new areas to spread out, the speculators were getting closer to Billy's front door.

Billy watched some of the new development from afar. It had crept along the western edge of the Columbia, heading in an easterly fashion. He thought it would not be long before it was gaining on him, edging him out and farther into the sagebrush country behind him. So this was Billy's plight: a hardscrabble living, close to the river of his dreams. He shared this life with the few close friends who would drop by from time to time, reminiscing with them about the old times, often in an inebriated state after the first case of beer. It was in this frame of mind that he told a few old friends of his dreams. Seeking solace or requiem, he shared with them the recurring dream that great waters advanced, moving rapidly and gathering up all manner of man and beast as they sought their level and beyond. The friends listened, laughed heartily, and left Billy to his dreams.

37. Visitation

DAVE HAD BEEN SPENDING MORE and more of his free time with the boys, thinking nothing of jumping into the car and making the hour's drive just to spend a little extra time with the kids. He also had been battling with his ex on visitation, going back and forth with his lawyer and trying to gain some foothold that would allow him to be more than just a telephone dad. The court system was a formidable opponent, along with his wife, and he often felt more than just a little intimidated by a system that did more for the mother's rights than the father's. The cards, after all, were stacked in her favor; she got the children, the support, and in several states alimony also. Dave often felt frustrated with the lack of recourse available to him. His lawyer, an associate in a large firm, always seemed to be too busy. It was often difficult to get an appointment scheduled that would not interfere with either his work schedule or the many court hearings and appointments that his lawyer had scheduled. Dave was finding himself lost in a legal jungle and growing more discouraged with the legal bureaucracy. For the time, the boy's mother did let their father see them almost as often as possible, but Dave never really knew how long that would continue. He suspected that it might even be a feint to catch him off guard so that she would gain even more control of their children's destiny. Dave decided not to preoccupy himself with those thoughts, however, and instead to focus on the day-to-day parenting available to him.

Dave was often taking the anger and the hopelessness of his situation into the office. Somehow he was able to pull it together while faced with the often daunting tasks that his position required, focusing his entire being on running a system that provided electricity for millions of northwestern homes. He was able to work through the up and downs of his wife's fickle behaviors. In the evenings after work, if he decided to forego the drive to see the kids, he would often go out with a few of his friends for a few beers and a chance to leer at the local beauties. A few times, he even benefited from these outings with a one-night stand, but such occasions were rare. He always had fears in the back of his mind of picking up a disease or some virus that could end his life and leave his children without a father. More often than not, he declined the temptations that always seemed within his reach. He kept his forays out on the town to a minimal number, suspecting that the night living would too easily become a habit and not wanting to lose his edge at work.

Dave was able to set up a rudimentary schedule with Sharon; she had decided that alternating weekends and a couple of days during the week would suffice for all the paternal needs of the boys. They did not have a court date, and both of them opted to avoid that at least temporarily to avoid the cost of litigating. They found themselves in agreement, at least for now, on the welfare of their children; the technicalities would be ironed out later. Dave again was able to focus on his work with the brief respite that he was now getting from Sharon. This allowed him to return to some old dilemmas and work his way through the future problems that by and large he knew would present significant problems in the future.

38. Dave's Distractions

THE ELECTRIC INDUSTRY WAS COMING into the twenty-first century, and with the transition came all manner of new philosophies, many of these promoted by greed in the boardroom. Dave watched the future of the BPA also change. It fought with environmentalists who felt that it was fundamental to the ecosystem to breach some of the dams on the Columbia, allowing the return of spawning salmon back to their ancestral birthplaces. Dave found himself in agreement with some of the arguments, but he also knew the price of progress. In the end, the stock analysts, shareholders, and management would win any round with the environment people, save for a few encounters with the lawyers in various courtrooms throughout the state. Dave had many distractions, and in the meantime the Y2K enigma was constantly plaguing him. He worked through the many possibilities and scenarios that could hinder or render useless all the power grids providing energy to the Northwest. Somehow, with the joint effort of others in the field and the company's elaborate systems of backups, it looked like the BPA would come into the year 2000 with only a few minor difficulties. Dave was not content; several months had passed since the virus that had caused so much havoc had made its appearance. No one had been apprehended, and although the search had continued, it had floundered. Somewhere, Dave suspected, whoever was responsible was lying in wait, and when least expected would again make his presence known. Dave shuddered at the premonition.

39. Psychosis

CHRIS ENTERED THE WORLD OF insanity slightly sedated from a combination of Ativan and Haldol. After the doctor had heard the evidence against Chris and his bizarre behaviors, it was purely by rote that he signed the commitment papers and, with the acquiescence of Chris's parents, gave the go-ahead for further inpatient hospitalization. Chris, even in his psychosis, understood the gravity of the events that had unfolded in the emergency room. He went berserk, overturning litters and running through the halls of the emergency room, pushing past staff and patients until he was finally subdued by several orderlies and a few young male residents. His flight for freedom ended several feet from the doors that led to the street. Upon capture, he was immediately given the IMs, one of Ativan and the second a cocktail of Haldol and Cogentin. The shots were sufficient—and immediate. Chris felt a strange calm creep upon him. His world was almost fantasy-like as some of the young men who had earlier wrestled with him now talked to him in soothing tones of voice. They dexterously moved him to a litter and strapped him securely in place for his future destination of Western State Hospital. He smiled up at his captors, tried to mouth words that would not flow over his lips, and then stared unblinking into the myriad lights that passed before him as they hustled him off to the waiting ambulance that would take him into the night. He heard the doors close behind him. The ambulance crew mumbled to one another, and Chris strained to decipher their language. He was having trouble understanding them; he was hearing his own voices, which were reverberating at a steady, even tempo, telling him how useless he was and that there was no hope. This was the world Chris had entered on that glorious June night.

The rest of the ride was quiet. Chris, feeling the effects of the Haldol, began to surrender to its hypnosis. He watched the streetlights as they passed by, counting and recounting them until his lids grew heavy with the sleep he needed. Behind the ambulance, Chris's parents followed. They consoled each other to the point of exhaustion, unsure if the decision they had made would remedy the current state of events. They finally acknowledged to one another that everything was out of their hands and was out of control. They soothed each other's feelings, gaining strength and the momentum needed in such a major crisis in life as this was.

The trip lasted for a good hour. Ambulance and personnel wound through busy city streets and through busy intersections, heading east out into the suburbs of Seattle. They passed expanding neighborhoods and along Lake Washington, following I-90 and then heading toward the Cascades. Somewhere in the night, they took a nondescript exit that led down a two-lane road for several miles and finally arrived at an imposing structure that would be the final stop in this night's journey: the state hospital. Chris was awakened by the stopped vehicle, there was peace in its movement, and gentle rocking and swaying when they were in transit. The ambulance crew had been professional; they kept their speech muted as to not disturb their wary passenger, and the ride had been without incident.

The two male ambulance attendants quickly got out of the ambulance after they had parked. The vehicle stood only feet away from large sliding doors that the newest patient would be wheeled through. The driver was well versed in this area of operation; he quickly went to a buzzer on the door and rang the bell, allowing the staff inside to acknowledge his arrival. He then proceeded inside with the signed commitment papers, Chris's deliverance from freedom into the labyrinthine world of mental illness. The other ambulance crew member patiently waited outside while the papers were being read over and checked for inaccuracies. He smoked a cigarette and thought about what the rest of the night would bring. Chris's parents parked several feet away from the main driveway leading up to the facility. They watched as the driver came back out of the hospital with other personnel. Then he approached the ambulance and opened the rear doors, sliding out the litter bearing their son and then removing it and slowly progressing toward the entrance. Chris disappeared to the inside. His parents sat outside for several minutes until they felt the courage to pursue their son into this latest chapter in his life—and theirs.

The parents were greeted inside by yet another doctor. He gave them a briefing of their son's whereabouts and encouraged them to see Chris but to not linger. He advised them to make their visit short so as to not arouse further incident or mayhem. After all, Chris was now considered mentally unstable. Husband and wife slowly walked down the long, cool hallway, which led to where Chris was beginning the process of being admitted. There was uncertainty as to the length of stay that Chris would be actually given. As in many states, this determination came with time and after routine assessments by doctors, nurses, and ancillary staff. Chris was now in a legal limbo.

His parents stood nearby, disheartened with the scene that was unfolding in front of them, Chris seemed to be in a state of sedation mixed with paranoia. The sedating quality of the Ativan and Haldol left Chris in a state of total helplessness; he rolled his head from side to side. He still was secured to the litter but made slight and futile attempts to release himself from his incarceration. He opened his mouth several times, attempting to mouth something to whoever would listen, but he was incapable of articulating anything that was intelligible. This is what Chris's parents saw as the hospital personnel got Chris ready for the final phase of his admission into the hospital. The nursing supervisor, who always seemed to be present at these events, looked on with reserve. He watched the proceedings almost with stoicism, waiting for the moment that would prompt him to turn to the parents and gently urge them to return home. This would save them the embarrassment of watching their son be taken to yet another exam room to be strip searched. The parents understood; they quietly gathered their belongings, which they had draped over a chair, and watched as Chris was released by his jailers and led quietly away for the search. No good-byes were offered; instead, Chris's father left some money for phone calls when Chris was able to talk again and nodded to all those present in the anteroom. They left quietly, returned to their car, and made the long drive home without uttering a word between them.

Chris was a cooperative patient; the search was done quickly. Jewelry and other sharp items that had no value were sent home with his parents. Chris found himself in the uniform of hospitals: a baggy set of scrubs with some booties. They wasted no time in devaluing his independence. His shoes also went; all his clothing was stacked, labeled, and put away until the doctors decided on his frame of mind and the degree to which he would be able to regain pieces of his identity. Chris found the whole process intimidating and strange. He couldn't understand why it was necessary to take his shoes also. After all, they made no statement. In fact, they were well worn. Later he was told that the shoelaces posed a threat to his safety. Due to his involuntary status, he was considered a danger to himself and others. There was no need for shoes.

Chris had finally entered into hospitalization. He was walked to the ward where he would be living for the next several weeks. At 2:00 a.m., all he could hear was the movement of the patients in their beds, an occasional snore, and then silence. He was oriented to his room, which he would be sharing with two other young men. Guided only by the light in the bathroom, he quickly found the empty bed and fell asleep. The following morning upon awakening, he was greeted by his new roommates. One was rather shy and isolated; the other talked constantly in machine-gun-fast sentences and at times made no sense.

Chris was not alone in his deficiency; he soon became acclimated to twenty-five other young men who were in various stages of instability. All were consumed by their deficits, and all yearned for the day when they would be discharged back to their independence. Chris's journey into night was not without pain and anguish. In the days and weeks to come, his assigned doctor evaluated him daily. Initially, the doctor ventured forth with trepidation. Chris, like all of his previous patients, was unique. The doctor was cautious not to overprescribe; he wanted to see some improvement in the young man's demeanor without pushing the envelope too far. He started early on with a small dose of Haldol. After a couple of weeks of this trial, he found that Chris had become sensitized to the medication. He had too many side effects, ranging from some irritating tics to the point in one instance of his tongue swelling to the point of gagging, which required a quick response and a intramuscular shot of Cogentin to reverse the effects of the potent neuroleptic.

Through all this, Chris's parents made the long trip out to the facility at least three times a week and every weekend. As the weeks progressed and the medications were changed, they began to see a small improvement in his personality. He became more outgoing and more conscious of his appearance. In the first couple of weeks of hospitalization, he did not bathe. His personal hygiene was lax, and he was disheveled. He viewed his family with the suspicion of a paranoid personality and shunned their attempts to reconnect with him.

In his attempts to find the right medication for Chris, the doctor finally settled on Risperdal. The dose was small, but in the days that followed, the recovery process began. This was what his family had prayed for. Chris was returning to their world, but release was yet to come.

40. The Army Corps

The Army Corps of Engineers were contacted in response to the findings on Lake Roosevelt. As an agency of government, it had a can-do attitude, whether tackling the flood basins of the Mississippi Delta or the extensive navigational waters that linked major waterways throughout the United States. The agency had been alerted of the findings that Kirk and his team had made in early July, and they also had satellite feedback and other information at their disposal. But they lacked the most important piece of the puzzle, and that only Kirk could provide. The engineers wasted no time in contacting Kirk at the site of the excavation. They insisted that he bring all his current diagrams and maps as well as any samples that had been excavated at the rift. They were taken at their face value, and Kirk decided to make the long trip to Portland on the following day. The day before his departure he spent scouring the site for additional clues that could provide some insight into the earth upheaval. Although the fissuring ran parallel to the lake, its movement had many jagged areas, with a peak-and-valley effect. The interpretation was ambiguous, and the more field experienced geologists racked their brains seeking an explanation. It looked as if the site were at risk for further separation or at least some major rock slides.

Kirk explored all these areas again. He had taken along one of the 35-mm cameras with a tripod, and while hiking along the entire length of the rift he stopped frequently to note where a specific landmark or one of the more unique formations occurred and snap a picture. In the end he had several rolls of film that depicted not only the length and specifics of the site but also the harsh and subtle gradations of rock and the effect of all this geologic movement on the area as well as the possibility of further movement.

Kirk had worked late into the evening developing many of the rolls of film. He decided to develop those that would provide the most explicit overviews of the snaking line from cliffs to lake, a sort of graphic silent film depicting various points of upheaval, geologic wrestling with the prehistoric mountains that had lined the lake for ages and saw change in epochs of millions of years instead of the decades that marked change in man's time frame. His work lasted well into the early hours of morning; he finished up the last roll around 3:00 a.m., leaving just enough time to catch a few well-deserved hours of sleep before making the long drive to Portland.

The Corps of Engineers had districts in Seattle, Portland, and Walla Walla. Each was responsible for major flood control, and navigational areas throughout the Northwest, and each was specific in its interests. The Portland office had a keen interest in Kirk's findings. Although the site where they had discovered the rift fell into the Seattle district's domain, Portland's concerns were more than just symbolic; they were justified. Kirk made the drive over the better part of a day. B the time he had made the long trip to Portland from Coulee Dam, he had slept for approximately three hours in the last twenty-four. He opted to make an accounting of himself at the district office, introduce himself to the CO, and then schedule any meetings or debriefings for the following day.

He met with the commander, an engaging man who had a ready sense of humor as well as a keen eye for integrity. He eyed Kirk carefully, already aware of his accomplishments and his background. Security had already checked through his records and given the commander a brief history of the man who stood before him today, for all of the obvious reasons. The information that Kirk would be sharing with the CO as well as a few other top brass was not the imaginings of a crackpot but rather hard evidence gathered in a hot eastern Washington sun that would clarify doubts—or raise more of them. Kirk found that the commanding officer was amiable and maybe just a little taciturn. He also felt an element of trust, so he was glad when the officer sympathized with his need for some rest and sent him on his way with a suggestion to stop off at his scheduler and get directions to a decent hotel and restaurant courtesy of the engineers.

Kirk slept well that night. After so many days of hiking and rummaging through the summer sun of the basin, he felt his old self again when he awoke. His muscles still ached, and there was still tension welled up inside him, but he knew that over the next few days he would be experiencing some relief of these symptoms and any other minor complaints that he was having. He showered that morning and shaved for the first time in several days. The only drawback was that he had no fresh clothes to wear to the meeting he had scheduled at ten o'clock. He ignored this minor inconvenience; after all, there was always aftershave to mask the days of sweat he had accumulated while deep into his explorations. In the end he decided that although his appearance would be a minor detail in the upcoming meeting, he would do some early-morning shopping at one of the local department stores prior to his appointment, at least to be more presentable. He ate a hurried breakfast at the coffee shop in the hotel lobby, found the local Penney's, bought a pair of dress trousers, dress shirt, and underwear and found that the hour was quickly approaching ten. He felt he was now ready to present his findings to the corps.

Kirk made the drive to downtown Portland in minutes. He had stayed in a hotel just south of the city, so after a quick jump onto I-5 he was soon turning into a garage, parking, and making his way into the inner sanctum of the commanding officer. Upon his arrival there were a few security inconveniences to take care of before his entrance into the CO's office. He was nonplused by the attention and strode into the office of the top man without hesitation or annoyance, like a man who was self-assured and knew it. Kirk entered the office with a briefcase full of developed photos as well as several maps rolled up under his arm. He briefly glanced at the several men sitting around a large conference table that graced the overly large office and was a necessity when any crisis had to be dealt with. He found a chair at the middle of the table, nodded at the men already seated, and then sat. The commander took a long glance at the men sitting around the table and then began introductions, Kirk sat quietly, listening as each of the men stated who he was and the district he was associated. In all there were fifteen people in attendance, and all of them were waiting raptly for Kirk's presentation of his findings.

Kirk's audience had already received a briefing prior to his arrival; they were not totally ignorant as to what had transpired, but they all needed more input. They could not enter into a blind alley without some form of illumination. Kirk waited until he was assured that all eyes and attentions were upon him. He then opened up his briefcase and methodically set out dozens of photographs, all numbered and in order. He took the several maps that he had brought with him and placed them on a large dry-erase board so that all could observe without hindrance. He then began his explanations.

First he summarized his first and current visits to the Columbia by pointing at various areas of reference where the rifting had been first observed. He did this with a pointer that had been supplied to him at the beginning of the conference. He made sweeping motions to indicate the extent of the fissure, to give it some sort of scale. Then he proceeded on to the other maps to indicate the other anomalies that had been found over their sleuthing, and last he approached the largest of the maps. This was of the greatest interest. Kirk, not one to be at a loss for words, detailed the shoreline. Then he indicated the long parallel separation that ran the length of the lake before finally disappearing under the water and into the limbo of the lake's depths. On the map several kilometers upstream stood the Grand

Coulee Dam. It was only a long vertical line with its degrees of longitude and latitude, but they could all see that the distance from rift to spillway was one of great concern. The men all went up to the maps to survey what was presented to them. Then they returned to the large conference table in order to view the photos that Kirk had so neatly set up. They were able to see the physical beauty of the site as well as conceptualize what the earth had rendered. They had hard evidence before them.

Each man spent several minutes looking over the photos. The pictures lacked nothing in detail; the latest technology had been applied, and their definition was beyond reproach. Kirk looked on as the district brass milled about, each man gaining from his own innate experiences in dealing with the unknown and the potential of calamity. He waited till every last man had returned to his seat before he again resumed the floor with more of the physical findings.

41. The Bellwether

KIRK HAD NEVER EXPECTED SUCH a rapt audience. He waited as men went to a refreshment table to refill cold coffees or water glasses before again turning their attentions to his briefing. The men listened intently as Kirk proceeded to give his account of the site. Over the several days that Kirk and his team had been at the site, they had viewed the fissure from several perspectives. With a little geometry, Kirk was able to give a precise accounting of what he and his team had encountered over the ensuing summer months. He summarized all the information over several minutes and then waited for questions. There was much concern displayed on the faces of the men present at Kirk's conference. The questions were all geared to what could be the widespread catastrophe in the face of further movement by the rift, whether there had been any further movement, and where the actual movement began.

Kirk was unable to alleviate any of their apprehension. After all, the sole purpose of his being there had been the extension of the rift itself; it had made significant progress from the time that Kirk had first observed it. He was candid with all those present. He did not want to be an alarmist, but an event of this magnitude needed not only further study but also contingency plans in place by all of the proper agencies and, in a worst-case scenario, a full-scale evacuation plan. None of his poignancy had been lost on his audience. After having all their questions answered, they felt they had heard and seen enough to conclude that they would have to immediately take a closer look at the site. The corps of engineers would now have to evaluate and coordinate efforts to stem the possible disaster.

Kirk wrapped up his morning's work. He then went around the room and answered a few more questions before excusing himself from what had become a stressful and draining day. He left the meeting, walked to the garage, and finally saw the sunlight that had remained hidden from him so much of the day. He felt overwhelmed. He drove back to the hotel and, after returning to his room, lay down and thought out the nature of the problem that was facing not only his unique team of men but all the other agencies that would have to be involved. It was fateful. If only the earth's movement could have been a little farther south, north or west! Instead it had found its mark hard in the basin and coulees of central Washington. With that thought, Kirk drifted off into a long and fitful sleep.

42. Casper

Casper had been having a tumultuous summer. The residual effects of the stroke had been bothersome. His handicap had compromised his stamina and at times was overwhelming. His sons, watching his progress along with his setbacks, knew when to give the old man a wide berth and let well enough alone. With the physical limitations and other negatives that Casper had suffered with the stroke came a newfound independence for the Henderson boys. They were now making all the routine decisions without the contributions of their father. The turn of events had come almost insidiously; after Casper had returned from the hospital, he was unable to be an active member in discussing the farm business. He was barely able to talk with the aphasia, so Jake and Keith found themselves not only planning the crops and deciding what bills to pay but also usurping the powers that once fallen on the patriarchal shoulders of Casper. Casper, even in his helplessness, could see that he was losing his usefulness. As the weeks advanced well into the summer, he grew increasingly weak. His sons watched the transformation that began gradually and finally became more obvious in the middle of July. The strength that had driven their farm for so many years was finally yielding its grip. The brothers decided that they would have to take Casper to the doctor before he lost any more of his strength.

In the last week of July, the sun had grown hot and without respite. Casper, who continued to be plagued by his recent turn with illness, sought some measure of comfort in a house that was poorly equipped to provide him with even the most minimal of necessities. The house had no air conditioning; fans had been strategically placed throughout all the rooms, but they only ushered in more of the hot, dry, dusty air. This had taken a toll on Casper. His sons, after returning from a day's work, would find the old man lying down, exhausted from his daily routine of simply finding a comfort zone in the house. In the waning days of July, before they had made the appointment with a doctor in town, they could also see that their father had lost several pounds. The old man was losing his tenacity and his grit.

July was even hotter than the weeks that preceded it. Thermometers in the shade registered 102, and it was several degrees warmer in the open fields. Casper had spent yet another day in agony, seeking out some cool haven but gaining nothing but a small breeze that only momentarily relieved his discomfort. Throughout the day he had tried to drink several glasses of water, but often he would forget about the need to stave off thirst and avoid dehydration. His routine was easily broken by his weakened condition as well as the insurmountable heat. He was able to exist with the help of his sons, who checked on him at least every couple of hours throughout the day, encouraging him to eat a little something as well as drink some water. Casper only halfheartedly listened to their pleas and demands. Jake, coming in out of the field to check on the old man, found him in a stupor. He put his father to bed, and the rest of the evening became a vigil of two men watching over their father in his last hours of life.

The old man passed from life late at night. The signs were there: his restlessness and hopelessness gave strong indication of his lack of will and deteriorating spirit. He had lain down in his room in the early evening, still hot and sticky. Oblivious to the heat around him, he lay quietly in his bed, almost unconscious to all around him. In the outer room, a vigil was being kept by Jake and later Keith, after the remainder of the chores had been taken care of. The darkness fell softly on the end of the day. Stillness came with the evening, and off in the hay fields, killdeer called their lonely calls to each other as the night brought on its nocturnal creatures and stillness. Jake intermittently checked on the old man with Keith. Each brother took catnaps and then woke for long enough to see how Casper was faring against the passing hours. They knew that the end was close; they, too, had seen the depression and the loss of his vigor furrowed deep in the lines that ringed the old man's face. All they could do now was wait while death crept into their house to claim their father.

Several hours went by. Casper had been sleeping off and on. Once in his rest he had called out to his wife and then returned to the comatose state. At about eleven o'clock, Nora had driven out. Jake had called her earlier in the evening to express his concern that his father would not make it through the night. Nora closed up the restaurant at ten o'clock, chased off the few late-night stragglers who always seemed to be there, and made the drive out to the Henderson farm. She made the trip out to the farm at a quick pace. There was no traffic at this late hour, and for all that mattered there was never any significant traffic on the Royal City highway with the exception of a few semis loaded with hay, cattle, or fuel. She maneuvered her car effortlessly around curves and opened up on the straightaways until finally she caught her road and then a long, dusty gravel road that led right up into the Hendersons' front yard. She parked and then briskly walked up to the front porch, where she was met by Jake. She could see the concern and upset in his face. He sat in one of the old, worn-out, rickety chairs, absentmindedly smoking a cigarette, looking out toward the fields and beyond.

Nora took her place next to him. She grasped his arm in a tender and feminine gesture. Within moments, she nurtured and cradled Jake close to her breasts as he began to sob from all that had been pent up inside him, as if overcome by the oncoming grief. Nora continued to hug him closely to her until the episode had passed and Jake was able to once again regain his composure. Within minutes Keith appeared and came out onto the front porch with tears welling up in his eyes, unable to speak for the sadness that had overcome him. He nodded toward the inside of the house. They all went inside. The dog sat quietly lengthwise in front of Casper's bedroom as the trio made their way to his bed to see that the old man had given up his fight, looking peaceful and serene. His chest no longer rose and fell with the lifesaving air that his lungs could no longer gather. He died at eleven thirty that night, with honor and dignity.

43. Death

THE THREE OF THEM QUIETLY went back into the dining room. The dog, once again, had taken up his post at his fallen master, his eyes watching the faces of the men and woman as they sat quietly around the dining room table. No one talked for several minutes; there was nothing to say. Only necessary were moments of bereavement to honor the dead and pay some sort of silent tribute to the man who had made an indelible mark on his sons and left them on a hot summer night. Nora spoke finally. She quietly urged the two brothers to start making their funeral arrangements and call the coroner. They needed to show his approximate time of death and the cause, and to be above suspicion. They called up the sheriff's office at 11:50, explained what had happened, and were told not to move the body, that a deputy would come out and that an ambulance also would be dispatched. They all went back out into the still night and waited.

They waited for what seemed like an eternity. The solitude and darkness were broken only by the faraway glimmering stars and twilight. The air around them was still and enveloping, almost like a protective shroud to ward off the dangers that surely awaited them in the darkness. Occasionally a faraway howl of a lone coyote would break the stillness. Then once again they were caught up in their thoughts and memories of Casper's life. An hour passed. Finally in the gloom that they had all shared came the first signs of activity: a sheriff's cruiser came toward them, its lights blinking red and blue. It raised dust in its progress up the driveway and finally lurched to a stop in the front yard. Two men got out. They were official-looking, starched, and wearing the solidity of men of their profession, suspicious of all the natural and the unnatural. They quickly made their way up to the porch and the three people who looked quietly on. The driver, a young man, trim and fit and wearing his holstered 9-mm, made the first inquiry. He asked where the body was and if there had been foul play. He followed up with the fact that the coroner was on the way and said that the family might want to release the body to one of the local morticians in town for funeral arrangements.

Although the officers were curt in their demeanor, Jake, Keith, and Nora felt relieved in their presence. The officers bore a dignity of sorts, and the brothers allowed the officers to enter the house and peer in on the earthly remains of Casper in his eternal rest and silence. The officers appeared satisfied; it was a formality only but one that could not be overlooked, especially in communities that were lacking law enforcement and where the ways of the West still prevailed. They were satisfied that the old man had died naturally and paid their respects to the sons. They stayed on until the coroner had arrived, performed his duties, and then left the family to once again ponder their loss. They later contacted a local funeral home. In the early morning, Casper's body was removed and taken to town for preparation.

The night went quickly after his death. Events unfolded and proceeded at a fast clip, and although the family grieved and cried much of the night, they still kept their heads and planned the burial and other formalities that they would be facing in the days to come. When the hearse arrived to pick up what was left of Casper's human remains, they stood teary-eyed and watched silently in their sorrow as the black vehicle made its long and meticulous flight back toward town on the dusty graveled road that had brought it there. The night by now had bowed to the beginning of dawn. Pink clouds formed in the east, and the first rays of the sun began to cast their ever-widening pall. In the chicken coop, the rooster began to crow with a strong and resonant voice, welcoming a new day and unaware of the night's proceedings. They all looked at each other, as if seeing each other's faces for the first time, and then sat down once again on the porch in a state of exhaustion.

The day would be a demanding one. Funeral arrangements would have to be made, but after the stress of watching Casper as he awaited oncoming death and all the excitement that followed, they all decided to get a little rest before the day proceeded. Keith went silently to his bedroom inside. He spoke little; conversation at this point was a brief economy of statements and yeses or nos. Everyone understood how the others were feeling. Jake and Nora chose what had once been an old hunting trailer that had been anchored at the side of the house for several years. It was an old Airstream, well used and worn. It had been somewhat reworked to prevent easy access when parked in the hills. Its windows had been barricaded to the point of a fortress-like look; there was only one small working window to the side of the door and another toward the rear, which allowed enough air to circulate throughout the small trailer. Shiny and chrome, it reflected with welcome in the morning light. During its days of hunting, it was often camouflaged by old military tarpaulins while it remained parked in an obscure spot under the trees. That was its history, and it served now as a place of respite for Jake and Nora, as it had on several previous evenings in the past months. They entered into its solid and confined space, opened the two windows, and left the door open. A fan served to keep the air circulated, and although it was relatively warm outside, there was a coolness inside that welcomed them. They quietly lay down on the single well-worn bed and slept for several hours in the arms of each other.

They awoke at one in the afternoon. Outside they could hear Keith as he worked diligently on a tractor, changing a flat tire. Keith had not been able to sleep; he got up and made himself busy until his brother got up and the beginning of the funeral arrangements could be made. They were both uninitiated in the task; they had buried their mother several years ago, but the ritual was arranged by their father. They were the mourners who watched helplessly as their mother was carried by six young strong men to her resting place. Nora had made arrangements with the café to stay on with the Henderson men; she had a replacement for the next few days and would provide the woman's touch to the stressful and necessary arrangements that would have to be made. Jake and Keith appreciated her helping hand. The demands of making plans to bury their father were arduous and difficult. Family members had to be notified. Casper still had sisters and a brother who had to be called as well as assorted nieces, nephews, and other sundry relatives on both sides of the family. They spent the following days with the help of Nora in organizing. They were able to contact all the relatives, and it had been decided that he would be buried on a Friday. The most difficult period was the trip into town to meet with the undertaker and select the casket and other items that needed to be arranged before the departed could leave this earth. They last met with the reverend and arranged for the eulogy. Their father would be buried next to their mother. This had all been time-consuming and thought-provoking. It was not easy to overcome the grief that the two men held in their hearts for the elder Henderson. They had cussed him often and reviled his obstinacy, but in the end they reflected on his strength and fairness to his two sons.

44. A Wake for Casper

Friday was a hot July day. The farm stood quietly, soaking up the warm rays of the sun. Vehicles parked here and there, and assorted cattle, pigs, and chickens milled about in their assorted pens, pastures, and hutches, almost respectful of the farm's loss. The funeral was to be at two. Little relief would be found in the drab and dark suits that the participants would be wearing in respect for Casper. Congregates began gathering at the Henderson farm the night before. Many were relatives who had traveled from other parts of the state or elsewhere, and the ranch was their hostelry for the night. A few even pitched tents or came in pickups with campers on the back. None were turned away; there was room for everyone who had come to say their last good-byes and pay their respects for the passing of the Henderson patriarch. The evening before the next day's ritual had not been dull. In the warm and quiet evening, the assorted Hendersons began to accumulate. They brought with them not only their appetites and road-weary bodies but also an incredible thirst. Many of them had imbibed along the highways that lead them to the farm, stopping at towns along the way to stretch cramped legs, let the children out for a well-deserved rest stop, and also get a cold six-pack to shorten the drive in front of them. The men and women who came to the Henderson ranch either were closely related or on the well-worn cusp of relatives thrice removed, an assortment of flotsam and jetsam who wanted to share not only their respect for the demise of an uncle or cousin but also the celebration and wake that often accompanied such an event. This gathering had promise early on, and as the evening commenced, the liquid refreshment did also.

Around eight in the evening the solemnity of the event gave way to raucous and loud behavior. Already the men had made the first of several trips into Royal City to restock the beer and hard liquor that were being consumed so readily and efficiently back on the ranch. On their last trip into town, they opted to forego the buying of cases of beer and bought a large keg instead. The several men who had made the trip into town all congratulated each other on their market savvy and good sense in making such a good purchase. They stopped off at a small store along the way and completed their shopping by loading up on snacks and mixers for the several fifths that already were quenching the insatiable thirsts of the mourners. On return the celebrants were jubilant; the beer, at least, would pour without constraint through the rest of the evening. Casper's death was almost a holiday in the eyes of his friends and relatives as the evening wore on to the later hours.

As the party proceeded and the drinking went on, so did the beginnings of conflict: an occasional snub here and there. As the keg fueled the silent flames, old feuds began to rise to the surface, as they do in relatives that had not seen one another for several years. Old jealousies were easily rekindled, and the alcohol added the necessary fuel to the long-dormant flames. The first of these pugilistic events started off with two of the younger cousins, who were well on their way to inebriation. They had not seen each other for several years, and there had been bad blood between them over a former mutual girlfriend. She had left one of them for more promising pastures with the other. They had set up a domicile together, to the dismay of the grieving party, and the long and lingering fires were fanned once again when they saw each other at the Henderson ranch. The young woman in question in the end had departed from both of the cousins, having decided that neither was good enough for her. That did not ease the long and festering hate that resided in the offended cousin. After several beers and a few shots of Jack Daniels, he decided the time was right to make amends for past differences. He approached his nemesis on wobbly legs and took a well-rounded right hook at his cousin, only to miss and get clipped with a left and sink quickly to his knees. A good man wouldn't have stayed down, though. He again found his land legs and rose to the occasion one more time to get a sound thumping.

At that point several other of the wake celebrants joined the squabble, many of whom also had petty claims of injustices done by others. Before long, an all-out riot had broken out among the twenty or so relatives and friends who had been socializing with each other only minutes before. The fights went on for a good half an hour, and the war injuries, bloody noses, and various welts and bruises were everywhere. After the fighting had culminated, everyone had seemed to regain a good portion of their sobriety, and all the simmering disdain and hostilities that they had let simmer between themselves were absolved by the melee. The fight had a purifying effect; it more or less was an escape valve to cleanse the air of old animosities. In Casper's death there had been a renaissance of feelings, and at least something good had come from his passing.

Jake looked around the open yard at the aftermath. He was angry that the fighting occurred but also relieved that several bloodied noses and black eyes had been the most serious of injuries in the wake of the event. He picked up a few of the broken chairs and other assorted furnishings that had suffered in the wake of the frenzy and decided to call it a night. The house was intact, as the bulk of the fighting had occurred outside on the warm July night. The combatants cleaned up their wounds, and most even made amends to their opponents. Not long after, they, too, made their ways to their various lodgings, A few laid out their sleeping bags under the open sky and quickly went to sleep. Jake and Nora quietly slipped out of the notice of all that was in attendance and went to the Airstream to get a well-deserved night's rest.

The morning sun crept into the opened windows and shined its first rays of light on the open farmyard. The night had passed quickly, and a few of the guests stirred quietly as they readjusted their bodies in anticipation of waking to the morning's callings. Many were starting to feel the first nudges of discomfort and soreness resulting from the previous evening's fanfare. Faces and egos were bruised. Many preferred not to get up to quickly but rather stay in the comfortable and secure wombs of their sleeping bags. A good hour passed before any attempt was actually made to get up and start the day's proceedings off. Men quietly crawled out of the sleeping bags and walked off into surrounding bushes or behind trees to relieve themselves. Then they stretched, scratched, and checked themselves to evaluate the seriousness of their wounds. Many had been lucky to not sustain anything more serious than bruised knuckles and a few minor scrapes. Several, however, had woken only to find that they were now missing a few of their teeth. So the morning started on that note. Hangovers abounded, and several had already vomited the results of their overindulgent night.

At a little after seven, Nora began breakfast for the many who graced the front yard and several who had found more adequate lodgings in the house. Mostly, the women had slept inside while male counterparts stayed outside. Nora watched with amusement as she peered outside into the open yard and watched as the men began to stretch and check themselves for the results of the previous evening's melee. She could see assorted injuries on many of the men. They all were rubbing and nursing various ailments, and some even spit out the remains of clotted blood left over from the previous evening. None of them were at risk for continuing on with another day of pugilism; they all were wane and docile, even courteous to one another as opposed to the fighting of the night before. Many of them spent a good half hour checking and rechecking their wounds, washing up at the outside spigot, and waking up after receiving the initial shock of the cold water. After the ritual of their morning toilet, they slowly gathered up their injured bodies and spirits and timidly, almost with trepidation, ventured toward the open door of the farmhouse and to their wives and women inside.

Nora had garnered the assistance of the females. Some of them had also been involved in the riot of the night before, but few of them had sustained injuries outside of torn clothing. They had chosen to do their battling from the periphery, taking sides with their men and lambasting opponents with whatever implement was within reach. After the blitz, they quickly ran off to the relative safety of either the porch or house and observed the remainder of the fight. The women watched with impunity and in silent persecution as the men slowly entered through the door. They shuffled in like so many errant children, having done some great wrong and seeking the vindication of their benefactors. They met with the deafening silence of their mates, who, although many had egged on their men on in the quarrel, chose to feel that they were wronged and ashamed and therefore would spend the next several days giving their husbands the silent treatment. They met the wrath of women scorned.

In spite of the aura of conflict and silence, Nora continued to unify the distraught females to help with the task of preparing breakfast for the many mouths and stomachs that were present. The fight had left all with an appetite, and the women, although angry and disgusted, felt the need to nurture at least when it came to helping prepare breakfast. Men sat quietly as coffee brewed and the beginnings of breakfast were prepared. Finally when it was served they ate ravenously, consuming eggs, bacon, and potatoes and washing it all down with cups of hot coffee. The men left after finishing the morning victuals. The women would again partake in a group effort of cleaning up the dirtied plates, resuming the hum of conversation they had shared among themselves before the men had entered the house. So the morning proceeded, and as the day crept closer to midmorning the women quietly headed for their husbands and boyfriends, once again to reenter their partnerships and prepare for the afternoon funeral of Casper.

At one o'clock, the family members had once again became a united front. The hours after breakfast saw a metamorphosis among all the relatives who had stayed over at the farm. The men spent much of the time getting ready for the solemn occasion that they would soon be attending. The women primped and preened over one another, and a stranger entering the Henderson compound would not have guessed at the goings-on of the previous evening. The transformation was incredible; men who had shared swings and blows the night before now were sharing pats on the back and laughing with one another, reminiscing about old times. They told anecdotal stories about the Casper they had known and remembered, none of which were lost on Jake and Keith. They watched the morning as it enshrouded the Henderson guests and relatives. The men who had fought so vigorously the night before shared humility between them as well as the hangovers that they would be nursing through the remainder of the day. And so it went, the culmination being the ceremony that brought them all together in spite of indignation, petty jealousies, and past feuds. The common denominator was the burial of Casper.

The afternoon sun rose high over the cliffs that looked out over the Columbia. In the open yard, family members gathered one more time before making the twenty-mile trek into town and the funeral home. The men, many dressed in Levis and their best western shirts and cowboy hats, stood stiffly, squinting hard at the sun as it made its descent toward the west. They muttered to each other in quick responses while the women watched for some movement from the Henderson men to indicate that the procession would be heading to town. Jake and Keith took one final glance at all the assorted guests, many of whom were sporting the remnants of old wounds, puffy eyes, and bent noses, and saw a ragtag group of men and women who in their own ways had respected their father and needed to say their last farewells. The brothers nodded in that silent western manner. Then both men and Nora climbed into the pickup, started it, and revved the engine to life. They gradually steered the vehicle toward the highway with the rest of the kin not far behind.

They made the trip in fast time. It was easy going in the afternoon, and traffic was light today. Many of the usual travelers would be boating and picnicking on the river, taking time off from work and finding relief in the cool waters, so the entourage found their procession unfettered with the monotony of slowed traffic and highway construction. They pulled into town slowly, drove toward the sole funeral home in town, and parked their vehicles in one long continuous line. Moving slowly and methodically, almost in a trance, they climbed out of the vehicles and made their way inside to the cool, air-conditioned silence of the funeral home. They all signed the guest book. Some ventured up to the open coffin and peered at Casper, silent in death's dance, seeing but not seeing. He had tousled gray forelocks and unnaturally pursed lips. Casper had lived life, and his relatives could not discount that. Regardless of any difference of opinions or values, they still thought of him in reverence. The afternoon went quickly after the eulogy. Pallbearers on cue removed the silver casket and slowly, in parade-like fashion, walked him to the open mouth of the hearse. Moving in unison, they slid the coffin inside for the trip to its final destination. At the cemetery a breeze had picked up, and this was a relief from the stifling heat. Those present listened intently as the final eulogy was completed. Then, silently as they had come, they left, moving quietly across the open field to their cars and the return home.

45. The Army Corps

The Army Corps of Engineers viewed navigation and flooding as the two hallmarks of their organization. They were responsible for not only the several dams that controlled the Columbia but also the many significant inroads that had been made in flood control on the Mississippi and the many levees that had been constructed to make that great river navigable and without malice toward the towns and cities that sat on her shores. They knew what an unharnessed angry river was capable of, the damage and death that it could bring without warning, so with Kirk's recent testimonial and findings along with the photographic evidence to back up his claims, they found themselves at a high alert. They formalized a series of plans and notified other government agencies that would require ancillary coordination in the event of a catastrophe. They acted discreetly, not to arouse suspicions and classified the plan to avoid the premature leaks that often accompanied government works.

46. Into Harm's Way

The corps started their work at the end of July. They had more than enough resources at their disposal to evaluate Kirk's findings and possibly alleviate any problems or future concerns. Several of the corps members had driven over to the basin area with large boats pulled behind sturdy four-wheel-drive pickups. They had already decided on a site that would be best for launching their craft without arousing the suspicions of locals, who often used the lake as their private fishing hole and were well aware of any unusual activity. The lake behind Grand Coulee contained a vast amount of water. At one point in time the dam had been the largest of its type, and she still held the record in the United States for the amount of kilowatt hours produced as well as the billions if not trillions of gallons of water behind her. The corps of engineers realized her importance not only for the benefits that this concrete monolith provided but also the perils she was capable of in the event of any catastrophe, whether manmade or natural. It was with this mindset that several officials and engineers had made the trek over to investigate her.

Kirk met with the engineers from the corps upon their arrival, he had already secured a sight where they would be able to launch their craft into the lake without arousing the suspicions of locals. There were always several boats in the lake throughout the day. Many belonged to visitors from other parts of the state who were camping and enjoying the benefits the vastness of Lake Roosevelt offered. To see a few more boats on the lake would make little difference to those who frolicked on her shores and on her waters. Not all the boats that the corps had towed would be in the lake; They had decided to use three unmarked craft which were large enough to accommodate divers and the technological equipment and support systems they would need in a venture of this magnitude. Other boats, smaller in size, would be used as backup and were to be launched during evening hours when things returned to their natural state of quiet. Kirk had set about with his team preparing the site. It was going to be a joint venture; because Kirk's team was already knowledgeable about the geographical anomalies, the corps had decided that the university researchers would be an indispensable component of the project.

The group in total was a ragtag small army of professionals that included geologists, engineers, and agronomists as well as the technical support staff and experienced divers who were required on a venture of this nature. They knew well the nature of what they were undertaking and mentally prepared themselves for the advent of the unknown. Their campsite sat well above the banks of the lake, where boats could be launched into the blue waters for their daily routines and observations. Over the days since the corps had arrived at the camp, they had monitored the daily activity on the lake and decided that their best approach would be launching the boats during the noon hours so as not to arouse suspicion or concern. They then proceeded along the shore, looking carefully through binoculars and sighting in on the large parallel fissure that ran its jagged horizontal course silently and malevolently along the lake's shore. Over the next several days, they stopped at various locations to let the divers jump into the crystalline waters to study the depths. For those who glided by in their craft, the sight of the skin-divers was a little unusual, but they took it in stride.

The divers continued on with the task at hand. They had little concern for the eyes that watched them at various distances and wondered what had brought them there. They had placed themselves in harm's way; the dam continued its daily workings. Water still flowed magnificently over the spillways, and that incredible current was always there to tug the unsuspecting toward its mouths and into oblivion for those who ventured within her reaches. The divers were well aware of the currents and undertow; each had safety lines tethered to him and then to the next diver. Their daily routine consisted of a dive in the afternoon, which would take at least half an hour or longer depending on the variables of current oxygen supply, water turbidity, and a host of other variables in addition to the weather, which was always of concern. The lead diver, a sullen man by the name of Preston, was always the first to go overboard with the other divers several minutes behind. He had preferred it that way, being always suspicious and worried that the waters would become murky if other divers proceeded ahead of him.

On the first of several days, he glided into the depths of the gray world, light in hand, and began an exploration of what at one time had been great canyons that loomed several hundred feet skyward. Then the dam had swallowed up these temples of rock and nature, burying them under billions and billions of gallons of water as they became a sunken cemetery unseen by the human eye again. He looked up and down the great crevices, silent but still deadly in their own way, standing guard over a river that lapped quietly over their summits. Preston made careful note of the juxtaposition of each and every one of these great canyons like so many characters in cuneiform, each precipice with a story to tell. His colleagues later glided toward him in the Columbia darkness, their underwater lights playing over the surreal world of the water's depths and then up on the high cliffs that once again might see the beginnings of daylight cast the long shadows across their walls. The divers were one now. Carefully, they proceeded several meters and began to see the great cracking unobserved from terra firma above. After brief minutes, they found themselves quickly returning to the surface and air.

The team that Preston had gathered together for this endeavor had worked with their leader many times before in every imaginable set of circumstances, some in their control and others not. They not only respected him for his seasoning and expertise but knew that he was a natural-born leader, someone who went beyond the hundred percent that was demanded of them in this field. He was professional and able to maintain focus on any project. Preston spent several hours after their initial dive sorting through the equipment at hand, which included various underwater cameras with excellent filming capabilities as well as the life-preserving equipment that they would all be wearing. He did this in order to ensure as much as possible a flaw-free system that would not hinder their progress in the days to come. It was paramount that each and every gauge, air hose, and oxygen tank be free of any malfunction. After he was satisfied with his own check-through, he left it up to the individual teams to make their follow-through. They all spent much of the evening in this manner until they all concurred that they were ready for the following day's work.

Day two began without fanfare for the diving team. They all finished their breakfast, eating hastily with long intervals between comments. Reflectively they sat and thought about what that day's findings would reveal, they all had seen the gaping maw that placed its geological fingerprint of the cliffs below the water's surface, like a large outstretched hand with an endless lifeline beckoning the deep to answer to its pleas.

They were excited and apprehensive as well as restless. All were master divers with hundreds to thousands of hours between them in the twilight world of the deep underwater recesses. Yet this dive, like so many before, was unique, and with its mystery was an air of fear, not so much of what they had seen as of what was further ahead. They all rousted themselves from their daydreaming and quietly went to their equipment one more time. They would check their hoses, gauges, and systems in the obsessed way men of this station do before throwing themselves into the laps of danger.

Kirk had conferred with Preston the previous day, requesting a debriefing of what they had seen under the water's depths. What he had heard was alarming, but anything to do with nature was pure conjecture and guesswork until all the evidence was in. At this point they were still in the discovery process and days away from making any kind of evaluations. They had decided that on day two they would make the dives in the morning on through the afternoon. That would give them more time to view the fissuring and the capability of progressing up the lake a little farther. The diving team gathered all their equipment together and headed down to the moored boats anchored close to shore. Rafts were used to get out to them; their larger size precluded tying them up on the banks. The boats were large so they could accommodate the various equipment that was needed to accompany the divers on their drops. The men eagerly paddled the short distance out to the boats and hoisted themselves and their equipment over the sides. They made preparations to start the engine and glide farther down the lake. The morning was peaceful and the lake calm; water lapped serenely against the hulls, and overhead blue skies and a bright sun were promise enough of a day that hopefully would bring answers to many of the questions that the team had been talking about.

The boats now began to motor along the shore, their crews looking up at the ragged cliffs towering above them and then looking at the shore to recheck landmarks from the previous day's outing. They continued on for approximately two miles, keeping the pace slow in order to fully evaluate outcroppings and subtleties of escarpments that might reveal further evidence of rifting and past quake activity. They finally reached their destination, several miles from the dam and safe enough for diving without the danger of being caught up in undercurrents. Kirk briefly gave the men an accounting of what he wanted them to look for. Then with a nod, he wished them all good luck in their pursuit.

Preston, as with previous dives, was first overboard. The shiny tanks on his back glinted back at those still on the boat as he sank into the blue depths of the lake. After several minutes, a second, a third, and a fourth diver all propelled themselves into the blue waters, leaving only the telltale signs of air bubbles that floated lazily to the surface. Below, the divers swam in a single line, each several feet behind the man in front. They peered out into the vapid waters, looking through the portals of their masks as they snaked deeper into the waters. Eventually they closed in on Preston, who had started photographing a long parallel rift that snaked eerily along the submerged cliffs. He indicated in various hand signals to the other divers the need to get some measurements. The men began the task eagerly and by the end of the first hour of the dive had been able to calculate a factual estimate of the depth and width of the fissure that they were now investigating. The length was still an anomaly. They still had to venture farther on in order to see if this great line would end well out of proximity of the dam.

They came up at one-hour intervals, pausing long enough to rest several minutes, talk over their finds, and load and unload film. Fresh tanks were the last element of their agenda. While they took their breaks, the boats would glide on up the lake, generally no farther than a quarter mile. Kirk sat stoically on the bow of the lead craft, ruminating between debriefings from the surfaced divers and piecing together in his mind the patterns of a large and disturbing puzzle. Each debriefing the men had given him wore the perilous cloak of past and future quake activity in the region. All the signs were there, and he was captivated by them.

Kirk waited anxiously as each return trip of the divers fed him even more information of the enfolding picture. The day continued through the heat of afternoon sun. Boats and water-skiers zoomed by, oblivious to the several moored boats with divers periodically returning to them. Kirk himself was unconcerned by the activities of the lake. As five o'clock came, they decided to end the day's dives. They had covered a huge chunk of territory. The divers took off the burdensome tanks and began the routine of removing all their equipment and stowing it for the following day. Kirk was relieved when they had decided to call it a day. He had managed to get a sunburn in spite of all the sunblock he had applied. He was angry at himself for being too focused on the divers during their drops to tend to his own physical needs. He knew that with his current ailment he would have limited capabilities and would not be able to accompany the men on future dives on the following days without risk of getting sun sickness. He acknowledged to himself that he would have to be useful in other ways.

The boats turned about, engines rumbling in staccato, and men, boat, and lake were one, each dependent on the others.

Slowly they all moved toward the west and back to the base camp and the familiarity of food, conversation, and a cold beer. The usual group of men was at the shore to greet their return, waving and motioning the first boat to its berth. When an orderly line of white hulls was lashed to makeshift moorings, the divers and crews disembarked. The men all greeted each other. Those whose primary mission was to decipher all the previous day's information and found themselves at the base camp during the day were eager to greet the returnees and pump them for the valuable information that would add pieces to the giant jigsaw puzzle that they were now attempting to assemble. They all converged into a semicircle, briefing one another on particular finds that were of interest. Then they proceeded up the rocky incline to the waiting vehicles that carried them back to the environs of their camp and their nomadic existence in the sandy, rugged terrain of the Columbia Basin.

The following day was a loss. Evening brought in large, threatening storm clouds from the west. Gray and voluminous, they pelted the tents with torrents of rain throughout the night and continued on through much of the day until tents, men, and equipment became drenched with the outpouring. The camp was now inundated with rivulets and small lakes. Men, too, were drenched to the bone, cursing vehemently at nature's wrath, and seeking out the protection of their vans and trucks as a last avenue of comfort until the storm passed on to the east. Men and machine now faced the indomitable task of letting nature repeal its destruction, and for the next couple of days they waited, reassembling the camp to its previous orderliness. Busily, they assessed their water losses and decided what they could dry out and reuse. Three days after the storm, they were again up and running. Eagerly, they prepared for Preston and his team to resume their dives.

On day five, inclement weather moved in. The diving team had one full day of R and R under their belts, having spent previous days in the mop-up actions that were a result of their battle with the heavy rains. Like other members of the team, they had to recheck equipment as well as make sure that nothing was so waterlogged that it would be useless in future dives. Their instruments were delicate, and subtle, unseen problems could mean life or death when least expected. They had met with Preston late on the previous evening. All his divers felt comfortable with their equipment, and each used the buddy system to confirm that all was well with his diving apparatus. They were ready for their most important dive. The morning was clear and the air warm and still. The lake began to shimmer with the first rays of light. The men had all gotten up early and proceeded to give their equipment another once-over before entering the beckoning lake. By seven o'clock they had conferred with each other on the day's agenda and what they had hoped to accomplish. They would approach the rear of the dam within a mile, well beyond limits regardless of the status of the spillways. The reclamation people had accommodated them in their plans, though. On the last day of their dive and probably the most important, all eleven spillways had been closed and locked into their positions. These mammoth gates held back the waters of a lake well over a hundred miles in length and backed up the Columbia well into the Canadian province of British Columbia. No guess could even approximate the sheer volume of water held behind the dam other than printouts provided by technology and computers. With the closure of the gates, some of the risks were alleviated, but not all. In the depths, large rocks and other miscellaneous items often moved about unaided. The divers knew this and were well aware of the many risks that they could encounter at such a close range of the dam itself.

 Satisfied with the weather and the relative calm of the morning as well as the lake's waters, the diving team gathered in a circle and, with Preston leading the way, invoked a prayer in the hopes of all the men returning safely after their dive. The men then busied themselves in their obsession of rechecking their equipment for leaks and failures before heading down to the boats and the day's adventures. They quickly stowed the equipment on board and waited eagerly for their companions to join them. Eventually all the boats were loaded. With high hopes for the day's dive, several others who had been based at camp now joined them as to not miss out on anything significant. The boats were loaded, and some were slightly over capacity, but nothing could deter the men in their quest. Men shouted over the churning Evinrudes. Arms waved wildly in the still morning, and the go-ahead was given.

47. Diving

Several boats left the confines of the small Getty, where they had hugged the shoreline, as more effort was being applied in looking at the magnificence of the canyon walls that loomed over their heads than in watching the waters beneath them. Eventually the lead boat began to slow to a crawl with those behind it obeying its silent command. They watched as it came to a full stop and then dropped anchor. After reaching the lead craft, the other boats followed suit, each boat a good twenty to thirty feet away from other crafts to avoid problems and give the divers adequate room. Man and boat now were silent as divers in slick black wetsuits began preparations to go overboard and once again reenter the dark world of the beyond.

Preston was ready. He had been ready for hours, even days, before this dive. Everything led up to this, and in a way it was a test of his skills and professionalism. He noiselessly went about his business, stretching his muscles and twisting. His mornings always started out with some variation of calisthenics and warm-ups to loosen up stiff muscles from a night's sleep, and today was no different. He always recommended that divers who accompanied him go through this routine, and they always acquiesced to his demands. He continued on through his machinations, fiddling with various nozzles, gauges, and hoses. Here and there he gave a quick tap with his finger and a discerning look before he hoisted the large twin tanks upon his back with help of another diver and then spit several times on the glass inside of his mask to get the clarity he would need once below the water's surface. Having finished, he then aided other divers who also were preparing themselves for the dive. They took several minutes a half an hour to get themselves suited up. The tanks and various other accoutrements that they took along with them were bulky and awkward; it took a degree of finesse in order to move around on land. Several adjustments were always needed, and the buddy system made that possible. Eventually, they got it right. Man for man, they were ready to take the next step. Glistening in black, tanks reflecting the sun's rays, they took the dive.

48. Under Murky Depths

UNDER THE MURKY DEPTHS OF the lake lay many unanswered questions that still gave rise to the apprehension of the team. How far did these rifts actually extend? Up to this point, the diving teams had been just out of reach of harm's way. With this dive they intended to come as close as possible to the dam's rear. It was a grave risk, and they all knew the danger of getting too close to the unyielding currents. They were killers all, subtle in rage and complete in the eradication of any who ventured too close. Huge boulders often rolled with the turbulence of these waters.

Preston, always the optimist, pooh-poohed some of the

concerns that individual divers had posed to him. Instead, he appealed to their sense of curiosity and adventure as once again they reentered the waters with a sense of wanderlust and abandon. Preston was first over into the dark waters, his body almost evaporating into the pool of water, silver tanks last to disappear. A glint of reflective light played back up at the remaining men and divers. He was soon followed by a second man and then a third. Finally they had all disappeared into the deeps of Lake Roosevelt. On board the boats, men watched the waters apprehensively. They cast their stares farther up the lake at the rear of the dam in hopes of seeing some of the telltale secrets that it had hidden so well. The waters remained calm. Nothing seemed amiss in what could be the most crucial dive of the several that they already had made.

Below the water's surface, men and gear silently moved forward, fins propelling them along. They chose each move with the utmost caution, lest they get swept up in the currents that always loomed as silent killers and be whisked forward in a gut-wrenching motion for thousands of yards and consumed by the concerted behemoth that fed the Columbia River. No, these men were professionals, and they slinked along close to the cliffs, eyeing each and every geologic anomaly with skepticism and detailed eyes. They proceeded on through much of the morning and followed the great fissuring that ran its jagged line along cliff walls horizontally, a great open maw with unquenchable hunger for the ragged rock that it cut through so easily. Preston and his team took several underwater pictures of the site as they proceeded, noting with exactness the location and other specifics that they needed for the team's chronicling.

They were several hours into their dive when disaster struck. Preston, although full of abandon for the risks that he had taken, was not without fear. As they approached the several-hour mark, the water became more turbulent. It began to swirl about them and tugged at each and every one of them, moving them helplessly forward to the unimaginable. Each man now became consumed in his own survival. They all began to retrace their routes out of harm's way, fighting desperately at the unseen enemy who so easily bounced them along toward an insatiable appetite. The men continued their backward progress in spite of the tremendous pull, many on the verge of panic. Somehow they managed to keep their resolve and maintain equilibrium in a chaotic world. They managed to eventually regain calmer waters.

A head count then was done. They had lost two of their companions to the blue-gray limbo they had spent so many hours trying to understand. They waited for several minutes, primarily in hopes of regaining their lost companions, but to no avail. Again the head count repeated their previous loss: two men were missing and presumably dead at this point. They returned to the waiting boats, all sunk into the sadness that accompanied the loss of friends and colleagues. They all reentered the boats, speaking little, and Preston gave the news to the men on board, although it was obvious that a loss had been experienced.

Over the next several hours, the diving team thought about their lost companions. Some mused quietly; others went into town and found local watering holes to forget the void and lose themselves in the quiet strength of spirit. For the next several days the camp was quiet with sorrow and respect, grieving and loss. Families were notified, and several days later funeral arrangements made. The bodies had never been found.

In the days following the drowning of the two divers, a coming together had been experienced. The team, now deep into sorrow for their lost friends, sought out each other for consolation. They grieved together and through it all gained an inner strength that was so much needed in times of loss. They united in their determination to not let the absence of the two dead divers prevent them from completing the project that they had all worked so hard upon. For the time being, though, the project was halted in order that the proper respects could be paid for their fallen brothers. So in the next several days, without bodies to aid them, they had to make preparations for the memorials. They sought out the families of the victims as well as their friends and others who had known them.

49. Without Closure

Several days passed. The families contacted went about making the arrangements as soon as the news had reached them about the two young men. Having no physical bodies as tangible evidence of their passing made it difficult to prepare for the memorials. It would have been different had they been burned beyond recognition or faced some other horrific manner of death that would have required the closing of their caskets, but that was not the case. Instead, two young wives and small children had to countenance the grim reality that they would not see even the most minute of remains. This was difficult for families that needed closure in life in order to distance themselves from the tragedy. The colleagues faced far grimmer probabilities; they knew that the lost divers had quite likely been pulled into that forbidden world that fed the dam's turbines, the penstocks. Nothing was said amongst them in their suspicions, and definitely nothing was told to the families of their fears.

The funerals for both men were on the same day and at the same funeral home, this had been done for sake of economy in order that everyone could pay last respects. The day was extremely warm. Mourners in black, some unaccustomed to the hot, dry air of the basin, grew fidgety in the small chapel, although it was air conditioned. The two men who had so bravely lost their lives were extolled to family and friends. The eulogy was delivered by a friend of one of the men, who summed up their brief lives and talked of the landmarks and families that they had contributed in their brief stays on earth. The men squirmed in their seats although trying to remain still. The dark suits and ties that many of them had worn made them uncomfortable. Women sobbed quietly and gently, now and then dabbing fresh hankies at the tears that they shed throughout the memorial service. It ended within the hour. The mourners quietly went forward to the families and extended their sympathies and hugs, shaking each other's hands. They then proceeded outside to the afternoon sun and heat. The men soon pulled off the ties that had constricted them and the coats that now overheated them. Women, too, removed some of the outer apparel that had proved to be stifling in the closeness of the funeral home. They all found some element of relief in the warming July day, and now many pulled out cigarettes and smoked casually as the last of the mourners filed out into daylight and joined those who already were lost in deep thought about the passing of their friends. Preston, too, had joined the group, but now his thoughts strayed. He paid his respects to the families, with brevity and compassion extended his heartfelt sorrow, and then left all behind. He was again submerged in that eerie world.

Only a few hours after the funeral ended, Preston was again planning how he and the others could further the project. He had foregone the wake that was to immediately follow the funeral in order to get back to the business of discovery. He knew that his teammates would avail themselves of the excesses of liquor, food, and soliloquies over the dead. They would be of little use for at least a couple of days while they recovered.

Preston chose to go this segment alone, and so he toiled through the evening piecing together the options that he felt were available and were the most practical. Several he considered were a little on the ridiculous side, but one idea stood out not only in its practicality but also in the risks involved. He had always kept up with the latest technology, especially in regards to dangerous dives, and it was in earnest that he became interested with the new robots that often were lowered to the inaccessible regions where no man could hope to survive. In the past several years he had watched the fledgling science become more and more developed, not only in mapping the ocean floors but also in exploring sunken ships. He had seen footage from cameras snaking through hulls and numerous cabins, revealing lost treasures that had been sunk in deep, watery graves for many years. This was the science that he felt would open up the lost worlds that he had so meticulously searched, at times in vain, and this was the avenue that he felt could assist him and the diving team in what had grown to be a culmination of failure.

50. Ned's Dream

In Kettle Falls, Ned would sit in the serene moments of the day looking beyond the still waters of the Columbia to the mountains beyond. The summer months had brought him the usual mix of tourists looking for ways to escape the stifling, humdrum existence of the cities that they had left. They saw the old man, a steward of approximately twenty cabins, as an antiquated misfit who filled evening hours with tall tales and the wink of an eye, as if seeking someone in the crowd who shared his secret and was knowledgeable without needing to quantify what had been said. The old man was indeed entertaining to the weary travelers who managed to stay with him while on well-deserved vacations. Ned, however, was not entirely focused on his duties as hotelier for those he served. He had become more and more perplexed about occurrences that he had seen on the lake. Often he would spend entire afternoons self-absorbed, and carefully he gauged the ripples of the lake with a practiced eye.

He saw something mysterious in the ebbing tides but could not quite pinpoint what it was.

He finally confided in one of his old friends, a Colville Indian who he knew might see some hint or telltale sign that could justify the gentle tugging on his psyche. The old Indian had by now become absorbed into Ned's routine of the daily ventures down to the lake, and they spent hours together on a hot afternoons sitting quietly by the lake up until the hours of nightfall, watching as waves lapped harmlessly at the shoreline. Today, the July sun had beat down on them unmercifully as they confided in each other. They both sat observing the nuances of the tide until, with an almost imperceptible shudder, they felt a gentle but strong vibration under them. The waves again lapped mercilessly at the shoreline, and a great silence filled the air. Even the boats did not seem to make a noise, finally a popping sound was made; it was faint but significant enough to be noticed. The two men looked quizzically at each other and then back at the lake. Now its whitecaps were blessed by the glinting light of the moon, and they kept lapping at the shoreline fiercely and rhythmically for a good half-hour. Then it all stopped abruptly, almost as quickly as it had started. The men knew this was a sign; nothing needed to be said.

Ned left his friend and proceeded up to his cabin alone. It was well enough into the month of August that the night air had a snap to it, a promise of the fall that would surely follow the hot days of summer. Ned looked back again at the lake and beyond. He wanted to make some sense of what he and Charlie had seen—some vision or the second coming? He shook his head. It was too complicated to understand, so he hastily went inside the cabin, turned on the light, and then sat heavily in his chair.

He sat quietly for several minutes, finally dozing off in a limbo of thought and confusion. He roused himself and then went to bed. He slept, but it was not the sleep of contended dreams. He dreamt of rushing water, of cliffs long covered by the warmth of still waters once again seeing the light of day and the rays of moonbeams. In his dream the water desperately sought its level, moving handily and with abandon down through the canyons and gorges that for so long had kept its currents in an artificial means of constraint. Its foamy fingers rushed over all manner of barricade and reached out well beyond its lines of demarcation up into the small towns and later the larger cities that dared to populate its boundaries. It was unforgiving in its quest and eventually gravitated to its source of exit at the mouth of the sea. Ned woke suddenly. It was only four in the morning, but he knew he would not be able to sleep again and got up.

51. The Columbia Gorge

DAVE HAD NOW SPENT HUNDREDS of hours looking through his systems for the virus that had infected the BPA. It was late July, and nothing more had shown up, but that did not soothe him. He knew that viruses had a way of reinventing themselves. The months of June and July had been hard on him; his only respite had been the brief vacation he had taken with his boys up into the Coulee country, which was relaxing but too brief. During the months that had followed he had found himself taking more trips up along the Columbia, stopping at the various vistas or driving up into some vantage point well above water level. He imagined the variables at stake if further spillway problems were to arise and release the billions and trillions of dammed-up water toward the cities and towns below. He saw a docile river below, but with the recent occurrence at Bonneville he knew the hidden dangers that lie behind the concrete walls that grace the entire length of the Columbia. He also knew that he would continue to look for all the subtle, telltale signs of a hacker who might have gone the terrorist route.

Dave spent an inordinate time focused on the river and its subtleties. After making several trips up the Columbia Gorge and well beyond, he started to take an inventory of various locations of concern. He mapped sites of towns and their position to the rivers and lakes that formed behind the multiple dams. He made reference to their elevations on the river itself and looked at the highways that hugged the river. He took note of the arterials that led up and away from the river and onto higher ground. He was not relieved with the discoveries he had made; in the event of flooding along the river, there were too few escape routes. Only at infrequent intervals was there any chance of actually driving away from the river. The highways that followed the river on either the Washington or Oregon side of the Columbia had only a few main routes that led away from the river and into the states' inland empires. Anyone who was close to the river and miles from these highways would not have sufficient time to escape the chaos of marauding waters that could quickly inundate miles of land and sweep any unsuspecting populace out to the sea and beyond.

Dave, having expended so much time and effort, saw that there was indeed great risk involved in living so close to the water's edge. The single occurrence at Bonneville did not alleviate any of his fears. The time he spent on his off-hours leisure trips up the Columbia offered him the chance to come to the grim conclusion that extracting thousands of people from the cities and towns along the river would be difficult, to say the least. His concerns were many; he felt that it was just a matter of time before another incident would occur, perhaps farther up the Columbia. With that would come a domino effect, a sort of perpetual motion of water seeking its level and proceeding down its path with abandon, stopped by nothing. Dave visualized this, and he thought that some government agency should at least be aware of his theories. Then it would be able to create a contingency plan in the event of a possible tragedy.

Dave at length remained tacit about his wanderings. To his coworkers he expressed only his concern that the hacker was still very much a problem, although nothing recent had infected their systems. They felt he was spending an inordinate amount of time driving up and down the river, and they could not understand his logic. Some thought that he was either fishing or looking for a site to build a retirement home. They never guessed the true nature of these day trips, but they satisfied themselves by assuming that this was just one of his quirks. After all, they all were guilty of a few of these themselves.

52. A Brief Respite

THE WEEK HAD BEEN BUSY for all of them. Dave's idiosyncrasies were low on the list of priorities with his colleagues. They all knew he was having a tough time with his wife and her daily demands and dictums, issued either through her lawyer or herself. They could see the stress in his face. Often he was deep in thought, and sometimes an element in his work would seemingly anger him for no apparent reason at all. They also wondered about his recent trips along the Columbia. His friends decided that on Friday they would shut down a little early, kidnap Dave from his thoughts, and take him out on the town for a little well deserved R and R. Friday was hectic; the summer had brought on its demands on the Northwest power grid. Air conditioners demanded electricity, as did the various industries scattered throughout the Northwest. It was a day of ebbs and flows and calculation, but eventually the men were able to sign off to their replacements. With a reluctant Dave in tow, they all headed out of work and high-stepped toward the glitter of Portland's nightlife.

They all went to a local hangout where many of the young

and not-so-young went to quench a week of thirst, well away from the myriad stresses and demands of daily work. The bar was an odd mix: all economic facets were represented, young and middle-aged, professional and blue-collar, some on the fringes, and always women, many of whom were single and often accompanied by their girlfriends. When Dave and his buddies arrived, the crowd inside was already well into happy hour. Conversation was upbeat, with frequent laughter and joking. Dave felt comfortable with the atmosphere, and as they proceeded further into the environs of the establishment, he felt a little relieved that his friends had insisted that he go out with them for the evening. They finally found an open booth by a window. It would not have been much longer until there was standing room only. Some of the folks who had gotten out of work a little later were now standing at the bar, drinks in hand, surveying the room for an open seat.

Dave and the guys sat and ordered their drinks. They all were checking out the atmosphere, looking at the prettier females and evaluating whether they were with dates or solo. Their attentions turned back to the table when their drinks arrived, and the evening began on that note. The men sat for the next couple of hours, making conversation and occasionally leering at this or that female, hoping to catch a stray look, but always keeping their attention on what was being said by their colleagues.

Jim, who was the most forward of the coworkers, was first to broach the topic of Dave's mysterious moods. The couple of hours of drinking were now having an effect on the crowd. They were no longer as inhibited, and the conversation a little loose. Jim without warning fired his shot, curious about all the trips up the Columbia that Dave had been taking and wondering what it was all about. Dave himself was caught off guard. Even in the alcohol's afterglow he was still a little reluctant to give any credence to Jim's question, but without lengthy pause he looked around the table and then quietly fingered his glass, running his finger around the opening as if searching for the answer. He finally looked up at their faces and slowly laid out to them his theories.

Dave had always been the quiet one of the group, always the listener, but he now had a rapt audience. As he sat with his friends, he gave an accounting of his findings and concerns, starting with the first sign of the hacker and then the Bonneville incident. His friends sat quietly, occasionally lifting their glasses to their mouths and drinking in such a manner as to not interrupt the content of what Dave was revealing to them. The men listened as Dave gave a full accounting of what he had been able to surmise, each sobering up after hearing the information and remaining silent when Dave had finished.

53. INSANITY AND BACK

CHRIS'S JOURNEY INTO THE DEPTHS of insanity was not without merit. He had been able to meet a few new friends, who he felt shared his own enthusiasm and spirit in regards to what he had been able to pull off. He never mentioned his actual involvement into the viral implant that had caused such confusion in the BPA's systems, but in the inane conversation so often shared by the mentally incompetent he would often intone his own spin on a particular farfetched idea. Chris and his newfound hospital friends spent long hours when not attending the various groups pursuing dreams of uniting on the outside and accomplishing some great deed or other grandiose plan—which often would be forgotten in the course of an hour. Although the men and women with whom Chris was hospitalized were often chronically ill and in and out of various institutions, he felt a great kinship for their ilk. After all, many of them were quite intelligent. If you could overlook the minor inconvenience of insanity and the fact that most of them had been committed, as had Chris himself, they were actually a fine group of souls.

With his small corps of friends he spent the next several weeks battening down to the routine of analysis, therapeutic groups, psychodrama, and medication, not in any particular order or with any firm frame of reference, and tried to separate the psychotic from the sane. His life would have been sheer turmoil had it not been for the other patients to whom he felt some sort of connection. Several of the inpatients had been involuntary guests for several years, sharing nothing of their dreams except the common denominator of barred windows and the occasional scream into the night's darkness, possibly to keep the demons at bay. This was the world that Chris, in the acute state of his psychosis, had the opportunity to share with so many, and it was a world that confounded him.

Chris slowly began to evolve back into his old self after a month or so. The doctor assigned to him had been making various adjustments to his medications, and after several tries he had finally settled on Risperdal. The medicine finally was paying off, and Chris began to articulate in a manner that often eludes the insane. His whole demeanor had changed, and his routine showed focus and goal orientation. This was what his clinicians had hoped for. They became enthusiastic about the change, and even Chris's hospital buddies—at least, those who were not gaining the same degree of change in their mental status—now grew a little paranoid of the new Chris. Although the metamorphosis was seemingly complete and Chris's parents begged to take him back home, the doctors hesitated. Turnarounds were often the exception and not the rule. They encouraged the family to leave Chris in the hospital a little longer. Chris would stay another month and a half before he would reach the point of discharge.

Chris felt that he had been making progress; he had been able to attend even the most inane of activities and remain throughout the monotony of these often too-long presentations without rebelling. He felt punished when his doctor told him that discharge was still another several weeks off, time enough to make sure that the medications were doing their job and that they were not becoming toxic to Chris. Chris saw this as a conspiracy; in his mind, all those who were on the hospital treatment team were conspiring against him, keeping him longer than necessary. He felt that he had proved over and over again his resiliency in the face of the mental illness that had put him in the hospital. He had a brief setback in the following week; once again, he became more suspicious of his surroundings. He thought that the professionals with whom he interfaced daily had ulterior and insidious motives. He isolated himself, refused meals and medications, and made personal hygiene a low priority.

Chris lapsed into this state for several days until even in the throes of his psychosis he was able to realize that he had to make the adjustments if he was ever to see the freedom of the outside and once again sit at his keyboard. The doctors who had evaluated Chris over the past several days once again saw an improvement. They felt that his brief lapse was a result of outside stressors that would easily be diminished by the return to a regular regimen of medication and therapy. Little did they know or understand their patient's resolve and willpower. Chris planned even in the throes of his craziness. The hospital had given him more time, and he obliged them by planning for his return back into the societal arms that he had left so abruptly. This included a return to the fascination of the keyboard and its power.

54. Under the Cascades

IN LATE AUGUST, THE PACIFIC saw calm. Storms passed over her, and fishing boats rolled gently on her waves with their hulls weighted heavily with their catches of salmon, crab, and lobster. The waters were warm and abundant. Storm fronts brought more rain than usual to the men who found their days at sea monotonous in between the runs of fish, and the fronts themselves moved easterly, moving quickly over the Northwest and dumping the remainder of these storms onto the Cascades and the cities and towns that populated the region. This fed moisture to the western part of the Cascades and wind and heat to the east. The Columbia, by its location, managed to benefit. It grew in depth and width and fed the lakes along its vast reserves accordingly. With this magnanimity of nature, the great ranches and farms of the basin managed to benefit in spite of the unforgiving summer they were experiencing.

August moved into September. Miles out into the Pacific, well out of sight and miles below the ocean's surface, heaving masses of rock began their brief primordial dance. Mountain slid against mountain, greeting each other with the heave of white-hot lava. Pushing and pulling, opening and closing, cauldron-like and seething with energy, the quake made its brief physical birth known. Miles away at the geology labs throughout the state and in Golden, Colorado, she was given a designation and a 3.5 on the Richter. Her real damage was additive to the previous quakes that already had left their calling cards. So as to not change the routine, she sent her serpentine fingers toward the east, pushing under the Cascades and toward the Columbia basin and beyond.

Once again, officials were faced with the quandary of determining the possibility of any damage along the entire power grid of the Columbia. This was no small feat, as the nature of the beast either could be surreptitious or blatantly obvious depending on the aftereffects of these physical disturbances. In the case of the BPA and the hundreds of men and women who monitored the power structure of the Columbia, it was of foremost importance to make quick and objective assessments of even the most trivial of problems. A pattern had emerged with the second quake: it was painfully evident that the centers were out at sea, but somehow the aftershocks had radiated several hundred miles inside the state and toward the Great Basin region. Management redoubled their interest in the Grand Coulee region and, knowing that they already had a team of divers inspecting the dam, decided to redouble their efforts and pull out all the stops, not sparing any expense in evaluation the area.

Dave, along with the other men in his office, felt the paranoid atmosphere that seemed to have surrounded them. There was more aftershock in the building where they worked than at the actual quake site. Tensions were running high. Dave and his cohorts were all overly stressed and overworked to the point of exhaustion, yet they needed to make sure that none of the grids had any inconsistencies or breaks. From a professional point of view, they were all detectives searching thousands of miles of electrical conduit, transformers, and rivers for that one insignificant glitch that could possibly bring an entire power structure to its knees. In spite of their exhaustion, they continued on in their long search.

55. Grand Coulee

Grand Coulee stood quietly in the mid-September night, bathed in blue light, her spillways all opened. Water cascaded down her, ethereal and magnificent. She put on a show for those who viewed her from the high vistas overlooking her and the swirling waters below her. Inside, men and women had once again been placed on alert, for been the third time in as many months. They would have to keep a close eye out for anomalies and trouble spots. They had been warned of the minor quake and its travels, and they had to be on constant watch. It was not the manmade so much as the physical world that could cause her great harm. In the bowels of the dam, a certainty of sameness enveloped each and every one of the technicians who manned her around the clock. The routine was boring, and the monotony was intense. Many found various ways of relieving the routine, and with this came a lackadaisical attitude that often removed men from their work.

Several days had passed since the initial warning went out about the recent quake. For the first couple of days, the workers inside the great cement monolith laboriously and tediously manned their stations, vigilant in looking for any small detail that might indicate a problem or a flaw that could lead to chaos. Having found the system intact, they grew relaxed, confident that the great dam was infallible, unblemished, and standing strong against the whims of nature.

Several men working the night shift found relief in a game of cards. The upper echelon would have fired the men instantaneously if they had known of the insubordination and outright lack of foresight that the card players displayed, but they didn't, Management was scarce at these late hours, and occasional supervisors were often part of the problem. On this particular night, the men had a furious game of blackjack going.

One of the technicians rotated back toward the consoles to briefly check on the many gauges; this in itself was a daunting task. For one man to evaluate so many variables was a fool's game. The men all took turns through the night at the consoles, but the money changing hands had removed them all from their stations.

They had greed on their minds, so it was no wonder that nobody noticed that a gauge that never fluctuated in a remote corner of the console now displayed an anomaly, its needle swinging wildly back and forth. After several minutes it stopped, nothing recorded. It had moved slightly. Later, after the technician that manned that particular station returned his eye to the panel, he immediately noticed the gauge's subtle movement. He tapped on it several times with his finger, but there was no movement. He thought better of reporting it. Even though the gauge was a measurement device and any deviation could be critical, he decided to let it go. It was probably nothing.

56. Lateral Movement

There had been lateral movement in the canyons and bedrock surrounding the dam—nothing significant, but movement nonetheless. Days after the quake there were aftershocks. These radiated underground, stretching and pulling, adding to the geological cracks that had already made their existence known. This was different; it was not observable. Deep in the earth below, it stretched under and beyond the dam, insidious and dangerous. It was not even felt, silent like the spreading crack of broken glass. It now was a sleeping giant. The one particular gauge that sat so lonely while its watcher absorbed himself in a game of poker charted the existence of the racing chasm, noting it by wildly dancing to its lengthening. When it reached its zenith, the bobbing needle came to a rest. It obeyed the laws of physical science and had done its job well. If language had been part of its attributes, it would most certainly have shouted at the men who had failed to notice this predicament.

Oblivious to all of this, the game continued until all the losers returned to their myriad dials and diodes, thinking about how they would explain their losses to wives and girlfriends and oblivious to the events of the night. The gauge sat noiselessly in its designated corner of the console. It had carefully charted and measured all that had happened, and it had done so to an absent audience.

57. Preston's Thoughts

PRESTON WAS ALARMED. THE RECENT quake, although considered minor, added grist to his mill. He pondered a thousand variations to the theme that was unraveling in his head: the large fissure that they had followed up into the point of losing his divers, With this most recent development, there were more questions than answers. Everything that had happened had done so in an uncanny sequence of time,: quake, quake, loss of his colleagues, then another quake. He almost felt that it was more than just a coincidence, that some curious and fateful turn of events was following him. He decided that he was becoming paranoid and had better things to do than preoccupying himself with the paranormal or his own neurosis. Preston had much to do, putting his own concerns on the back burner. In a few days, a team would be coming to the site with a miniature sub equipped with all the upgrades needed to assess the continuing crack. This included robotics as well as the cams and fiber optics that would relieve them of all the manmade risks. Essentially, it was auto piloted and accurate.

A single dirt road serviced the site at Grand Coulee. It was wide enough for larger vehicles but easy enough to veer off and immediately find oneself either stuck or rolling down a hill to oblivion. It was down this dusty road that Preston looked to see a slow-moving flotilla edging itself ever closer to the camp. Clouds of dust formed from the tractor as she effortlessly pulled the miniature sub on its lowboy trailer. Preceding her was a pilot vehicle, blue lights flashing their warning. Several lengths behind the trailer were more vehicles as well as another pilot vehicle. Preston watched in awe as the procession moved ever closer, ponderously. Sunlight glinted off chromed stacks of the truck, and the diesel engine answered the demands of its driver with snorts and belches as gears were changed. Several minutes later, the long parade made its way down to the shore. There was a substantial turnout area, so getting their cargo close to the water was not a problem. There was more than adequate room for the tractor trailer to position the load and then pull out without any difficulty. Preston waved the driver to a stopping place, and then the real work began.

58. Into the Depths

The arrival of the miniature sub had been successful. Concerns had been many, including the possibility of rainstorms, which could have easily hampered and detained the arrival of the truck with its precious load for many days. The road down to the site was considered primitive, and with exception of the manmade parking lot for the various vehicles at the site, could have been rendered easily inaccessible by even a mere hint of marginal weather. Luck was with them. Preston looked over the futuristic cargo and felt that the gods were with them here. He had the technology to explore the remainder of the river's depths without further risk of losing divers or endangering them. All exploration would be done from the distance of screens connected to the sub and its cameras as it explored the Columbia's depths, propelled only by commands given from a safe distance.

Preston caught himself daydreaming. He shook his head and, looking back to the truck and its load, saw several of the men conferring to themselves indecisively. Preston quickly looked around for the best spot for the truck to park, where there would be more than adequate space to launch the craft. He saw an inconspicuous spot and then immediately started waving his arms and whistling at the driver of the truck. The other men automatically deferred to him. He had taken over, and now the driver followed his lead through the semaphore of his signals. The tractor trailer backed slowly and deliberately until the rear duals almost submerged into the water. After several readjustments, the driver expertly aligned the trailer parallel to the shore and within easy access of the river. The driver and Preston exchanged nods at a job well done. The bulk of the work was now behind them. Getting the oversized load down the perilous road was dicey to say the least: each adjustment of the wheel had to be done with calm and measured reserve or all would be lost in a matter of seconds. Now the crew looked at the parked behemoth with satisfaction, high-fiving each other on their success. Preston, too, felt an air of relief when the sub was finally parked. Now came the unloading.

59. Billy Red Owl and Hoagland

Preston and his team were not alone. Several hundred yards away on a high ridge overlooking them was Billy and Hoagland. They had been spending the past couple of days on the ridge camping for want of something better to do. Gossip had made its way down the river regarding strange comings and goings up by Grand Coulee. No one was quite sure of what was going on, and a closer look became Billy and his acquaintance's only priority. They spent no time in loading up Hoagland's beat-up Ford Galaxy. Billy, without wheels, was at the mercy of his friends when it came to getting from point A to point B. Packing consisted of a couple pairs of jeans and sweatshirts, a coat if the evening happened to be chilly, sidearms, a shotgun, and a couple of cases of beer to stave off thirst. Edibles they decided to pick up on the way. They parked on a road which had led up from Banks Lake, several miles from their intended campsite. Both men were familiar with the area. They hiked for several hours until they found an area that was suitable to accommodate their four-man tent with a little extra real estate for a good-sized campfire. They set up the tent and went about gathering enough firewood to provide for the next several days' cooking. The fire would also give them a little extra heat when evening turned to the chilly side. Neither of the men needed luxuries; their lives were simplistic enough and free of frills. They could both manage with the bare essentials on this outing. Having set up camp, they spent much of the remainder of the day scouring their site for odds and ends, hoping to come upon some sort of treasure or ancient Indian artifact. This proved fruitless, and they gave up in short order. They drank several beers and then turned in. The following day would bring new quests to explore and maybe some invaluable discoveries.

    Billy was first to wake. He moved about awkwardly in the sleeping bag, eyes still unfocused to the early-morning light and head still groggy from the effects of one too many beers. After several minutes of squirming around in the sleeping bag, he was finally able to free himself and crawl on all fours to the outside of the tent. He tentatively stood on his feet, a little unsteady but gaining his strength quickly. With that accomplished, he was able to relieve himself and prepare for the day. Hoagland was now waking. He, too, was having difficulty with the cramped quarters of the sleeping bag and spent several minutes wrestling, wiggling, and cursing until finally he found his way out of the sleeping bag and the tent only to complete the same routine as Billy before him.

The morning was now gathering light from the east, and the cliffs below them began to show the first rays of eastern light. Darkness was nothing more than a thought. The two men now busied themselves by shaking off the remainder of sleep. They had brought two five-gallon military containers of water with them on their outing. Each had the task of carrying one container, and the hike to the campsite burdened with the extra load of water brought out several choice cuss words. They finished their morning toilet with little fanfare, washing their faces, brushing the grit of their teeth with fingers instead of toothbrushes, and, last, taking a few good swigs of water, gargling, and then spitting out the remainder. This ritual invigorated both men. They then busied themselves at trivial chores around the campsite, making coffee in a Folgers coffee can and sticking several slabs of bacon in the cast-iron skillet that they brought along. The fire had already been replenished with assorted sticks of wood they had found the previous day, and soon they sat down to the bacon, coffee, and a few hard biscuits they had brought along. They sat quietly, chewing bites of bacon and biscuit washed down with the strong coffee mixture. Each man reflected upon what lay in store for him, wondering if deep secrets were to be uncovered or some sort of secret scientific study was underway. Both men were not only superstitious but also fans of the supernatural, and both believed in all the mumbo-jumbo that they read in discarded *National Enquirers*. The day was already starting off on a positive note for the two men.

60. Watching

Now, men inspected the hull of the sub, looked admiringly at it, and gazed back up at the primitive highway she had come down. What luck! She had arrived intact. But on the remote highway to Coulee, the load and its procession of vehicles had been met with many a curious stare, this in spite of their choosing to come in early morning when traffic was at its lightest. The vigil of unloading the leviathan began in the evening. After the time that it took to get to the locale, everyone required a well-deserved rest and time to reconnoiter. A plan and contingency plan had to be agreed upon before any of the actual unloading. High above them, Billy and Hoagland lay on their bellies, as if scouting enemy troop movement. They watched with interest and occasionally humor as the men below moved about, arms motioning wildly at times to direct the actions of their teammates. They had no binoculars, but they could still make out without too much difficulty the activity as well as the hulking sight of what they thought was something right out of their scientific readings.

Below, Preston and the rest of the men busied themselves with the unloading of the miniature sub. All were oblivious to the interlopers who watched them from high above. Days before the precious cargo had even arrived, they had to use their creative efforts to come up with a makeshift pier that would accommodate the sub. This was done with several barrels to serve as ballast and to steady the sub as they guided her out into the deeper waters. The actual unloading was performed by a small but powerful crane. The operator watched the intricate hand signals from the crew below as he gingerly lifted the craft from its berth on the lowboy and then, with adroit maneuvering, carefully swung the mass delicately and slowly over the series of pontoons and an arrangement of cording between these in order to support the sub's bulk. The whole process from beginning to end took well over an hour, but it was a success. The sub finally was at rest, and although the water was shallow, there was enough of a cushion supporting it to prevent damage. Preston and the others quickly secured the hull to the floating pontoons.

Having at least another couple hours of daylight in front of them and a calm evening, they opted to tow the sub several yards out away from the shore, where there were deeper waters and less chance of a storm whipsawing the craft and damaging her. It was too risky to anchor her close to shore. Two good-sized boats pulled her slowly out into the Columbia; their progress was slow but steady. Well tethered, she followed the boats obediently, barely a wake behind her. Billy and Hoagland watched with delight as if they were an audience to a historical event. Their whole afternoon was filled with fascination and mystery. Below, as the boats neared the sight of anchoring, they slowed their engines and glided slowly. Although there was always concern about damage to the craft, that was the least of their concerns; she was well insured.

At seven o'clock, they had anchored the sub securely. She would not be alone, as one of the boats with its two-man crew would maintain a vigil to assure that no damage would befall her. The men would take turns through the night watching over the sub and its expensive viscera: a wide array of extremely expensive gadgetry and, for want of a more esoteric term, bric-a-brac. All the gear was finally secure. The sub floated benignly with its hull serenely enveloped by the improvised womb of pontoons, tethered to shore with heavy rope and watched by the two men assigned her. On shore, the others turned themselves to the vagaries of getting a quick bite to eat, a couple of beers, and some chitchat before turning in for the night.

They were not alone. Billy and Hoagland had not missed any of the details. Tired and hungry themselves, they edged back away from their vantage point quietly, so as to not reveal their existence. Their stealthy movement had not aroused any notice; they were too far away.

They both walked back to their camp. On arrival they grabbed a can of pork and beans, opened it, and ate with gusto, washing the food down with a couple of lukewarm beers. With fatigue quickly creeping over them, they quietly turned in, each looking forward to what the next day would bring.

A bright and expansive sun shone over the great coulees, men shuffled about meeting each other still in the early stages of waking, rubbing sleep-filled eyes, grunting, snorting, and farting. The day would be a scorcher. Those who were not in the environs of the miniature sub would feel the wrath of hundred-plus-degree temperatures while waiting and watching for the two-man crew to return from the Columbia's depths. Activity kicked off early, with the early heat already transforming itself into oven-like temperatures. By six thirty, not one man slept. All were milling about, checking over their equipment, and they wasted very little time with breakfast. Most would have some granola and fruit; sustenance was primary, and no time was wasted. The men all finished up and then made their vigil down to water's edge. Out in the cool of the Columbia they watched as the sub bobbed benevolently in the waters under the watchful eyes of her guardians. The men who had sat with her through the night saw the entourage as they gathered on the shore. They waved an acknowledgment and shouted. Their relief would soon be coming out to the sub to man her and launch her on her quest.

Billy and Hoagland, feeling the heat of the sun on them, grew restless in their tent under the radiant heat between bag, tent, and ground. They too were up and ready to go at an early hour. They were already feeling giddy, and the excitement of future adventure had left the two in a state of confusion. Both men hurriedly rushed around the camp, grabbing at various items, kicking over the coffeepot, cursing at themselves over their clumsiness, and trying to get organized. After several minutes, they settled in to a routine. Billy stoked the fire until it was warm enough to cook bacon and brew their coffee. Hoagland poked around for the binoculars. Finally finding them, he sat down heavily, looking on as Billy removed bacon from the pan and loaded it onto improvised plates. The two men wolfed down the victuals, saying nothing to each other as they ruminated in silence about what the day would bring. Finally they washed down the last remnants of bacon and grease with hot black coffee. Breakfast had ended; it was now time to get on with the day.

61. THE *PEGASUS*

THE MINIATURE SUB FLOATED LAZILY. The Columbia lapped benignly at her girth. Gently, the sub bobbed up and down as the men began to ready her for the day's work ahead. Lines were untied one by one until one last rope lashed to her deck was all that kept her captive from the freedom of the lake beyond. The two men who were to captain her came out to her in a small boat. They acknowledged the two men who had spent the previous evening standing guard with the craft. Words were of economy at their point of arrival. Having said little, they came to her side and quickly climbed onto her. They soon found her hatch and the snugness of entrance into her bowels. Billy and Hoagland had arrived at their vantage point minutes prior to the sub's crews being ferried out. They settled in, binoculars in hand, and quietly watched as the men on shore and those out in the river went through their routines. The two voyeurs watched with great interest as each man slowly hoisted himself into the sub. It was slow going in the cramped world, and the men slithered into her slowly so as to not hit any of the delicate instruments on board. It took almost a half hour until both men were finally safe inside. Then they gave several loud knocks on the hatch, and those outside checked her for readiness. Two men went over her carefully, searching for any signs of breech or potential problems. After satisfying their checklist, they returned the knocks. The two submariners would soon be on their way.

The two men were now secure inside. They looked over the sophisticated instruments. Both men had experience in handling the sub; they had logged well over the many hours necessary to be certified competent in piloting her. Topside, two boats made their way toward her. They would serve as tugboats; their inboard motors had more than enough horsepower to ferry the craft out into the deeper waters that would allow her to submerge without damage. The craft had a name that fit her. It stood in the bold script often seen in on exploratory vehicles of the deep. She wore her name proudly; she was the *Pegasus*, and she now moved with grace with her crew ensconced within her, stealthy and proud.

The enfolding drama was followed by the two interlopers. They watched as the glistening miniature sub moved slowly out into the deeper waters of the Columbia. The day was growing hot, and although many boaters, fisherman, and sundry other tourists would be recreating on one side of the lake or the other, there was nobody within the vicinity of the undertaking. The lake's inhabitants gave wide berth to what they assumed was some sort of secret mission, and that was all well and good as far as the men who now worked so tediously to uncover the secrets below the river were concerned. Outside interference would only pose delays and cause leaks to new agencies. Several days into their work, they had spotted a news helicopter from one of the local stations. No alarms went up, however; they never returned, apparently satisfied that it was a routine river study and not newsworthy enough to slot into the six o'clock time frame.

The sub gained her war footing well out into the vast expanse of the Columbia. She was a good couple of miles downstream from the dam, and although currents existed, she had the wherewithal to make her gains without a great deal of risk. On board she had the advantage of the finest cameras and sensing devices available to man. She also was well equipped with fiber optics as well as a transmission system that could send up rapid-fire virtual reality sightings in real time. She was a masterpiece of technology, and the men on the shore watched with a twinge of envy as she slowly sunk beneath the blue waves.

The sub's pilot was professional and calm. He gained his ballast slowly. The waters were unfamiliar, and piloting the vessel in the lake was like driving a racecar on city streets. The *Pegasus* was responsive to the faint movements of her joysticks she glided to a depth of fifty feet and then moved through the waters with absolute power. Inside, the navigators viewed the turbulence of the waters far ahead, using special cameras and lenses that could see far ahead of the craft. Luckily, the waters were not murky.

Their descent was flawless. The *Pegasus* was in her element as she pushed forward at five knots, not a breakneck speed but fast enough considering the topography she had yet to explore. The two men stopped the sub at intervals, looking through their electronic eyes and calculating the depths and turbulence of the waters that surrounded them. Delicate gauges indicated pressure and several other calculations, cameras revealed the cliffs to their starboard, and all the while cameras zoomed in on crevices and anomalies that began to make themselves more apparent as the two adventurers pushed slowly on. Topside, pictures from the sub beamed up onto the screens of several monitors. The technicians watched as frame after frame was sent up at real time so all could share the information being gathered below. The sub spent a good hour at the relatively shallow depth, and finally the team decided to have her descend further. She lowered her girth to over a hundred feet and was several kilometers beyond the base. Slowly the two men inside her moved slightly closer to the shore. The water was still deep enough and clear enough to capture the geology of the cliffs.

At a depth of 140 feet they saw the lesion, a great division that ran well beyond their location in a slanted, parallel fashion seeking river floor and beyond. They slowly pushed on, following the great chasm, until the sub became buffeted by turbulent waters. At that point they backtracked, removing themselves from harm's way, and followed the fissure back toward its origin. Al the frames had been relayed to the mobile unit, measurements had been made, and computers instantly absorbed, analyzed, and calculated all the data as they made their way to the information banks. Without question, the men had seen the potential of a savage earth resting in the shadows of Grand Coulee.

Billy and Hoagland watched the *Pegasus* as she submerged several meters away from the shore. The day had been sweltering, and both had the irritating sensation of sunburn on their faces and necks. They cursed the boredom of lying in wait as the men below spent the morning and afternoon hours in the odd-looking trailer with satellite dishes and other assorted junk that seemed scattered about. They were completely out of the loop as the submarine scoured the lake's bottom, and those who were involved with its progress spent all of their hours locked in front of screens, completely absorbed by the images being relayed to them. Billy and Hoagland knew that something was up, but for them it was pure conjecture. For all they knew, the men below were mapping out a marina or looking for some underwater Indian burial ground—something that was always close to Billy's heart, considering his origins. The two were patient, though, and as the afternoon hours waned they watched as the sub was anchored. Her two man crew carefully crawling out of her bulk, and finally several men quickly went out to bring the crew of the Pegasus to land. They watched the men with their binoculars; their faces revealed emotion and concern. They gestured wildly to each other, and one man who appeared to be in a role of command made a large, sweeping motion with his arm in a right-to-left motion, almost taking in the entire breadth of the cliffs before him and then dropping suddenly at the first hint of water. Billy and Hoagland watched the scene with confusion mixed with a little apprehension and fear. They decided that they had seen enough; what they had seen left them baffled. Both were silent on their hike back to the tent. They broke their camp on return, packed up their supplies, and made the long trek back to their car and eventually home.

62. Discharge

Chris, well into his third month of hospitalization, finally showed marked improvements. Over the course of his hospitalization he had several courses and trials of drugs and therapies to make an attempt to get past the psychosis that had prevailed. In and out of lucidity like dawn to dusk, he battled the dark veil of insanity with spirit and mind. At one point, after a brief treatment with one of several drugs, there was premature hope. Chris had seemed to regain his momentum and clarity enough so that even discharge had been considered. This was soon dashed. Again the mask of his craziness prevailed, humbling the professionals and others who had deliberated so passionately in their efforts. Finally, within the close network of the hospital, treatment teams met for daily reports on the inpatients, discussing individual gains and regressions. Chris often became the focus of their discussions. The psychiatrist who had treated Chris up until his second month was well respected and an authority on several therapies, yet while meeting with the members of the treatment teams he was finally acquiescing defeat in the treatment of one of his patients. Chris was battling for sanity, and now with his most recent lapse his parents had decided to request a change in doctors. Their plea was with substance and did not go unanswered. His doctor agreed to transfer the case, and the decision to do so was met with overwhelming approval. Chris eventually fought a new round with his psyche under the direction of a young and astute doctor from Canada, a maverick of sorts who believed in his own brand of dynamics and novel ideas and who felt that with each patient a new battle would be fought. He was no less zealous with Chris, and it was under his wing that once again Chris would regain his old former self.

Chris began to show some improvement in early August, although he had been down this road before. The team that was now in place under his new doctor chose not to rest on premature findings; instead, they trod cautiously. They had begun to use Clozaril for its antipsychotic properties, although its therapeutic properties had some significant side effects. They had arrived upon it through trial and error and a concerted effort. Chris was once again showing great improvement, and for the final weeks of his hospitalization he was monitored closely. Lab work was one of the prerequisites of the medication he was taking, and after days of reckoning and dosage adjustment along with the normal WBC counts required of his drug, discharge now became more concrete. Several more days passed in the slow world of inpatient stay. The doctors always acted with trepidation lest they discharge some lunatic into the public domain. That now seemed to be not even a remote possibility with the gains that Chris had made.

On September 3, a slightly heavier version of Chris took a long last look at the domicile he had shared so long with the other patients, winked at one of his roommates, and then proceeded out the door. He walked down the long corridors that had seemed so dimly lit when sleep did not come and, finally, out through the open doors into the courtyard. There he regained his freedom, by the good graces of the doctor who had treated him last. Chris was met by his parents. He packed his belongings into their car and turned around to take a final look at his doctor. Chris nodded to him and then climbed into the car. He sat in silence as his family made their exodus with their son.

Their trip back to Seattle was mostly in silence. Now and then the monotony was broken by an occasional comment by one or the other parent as they made small conversation about particular landmarks or reflected on the natural beauty of the meadows and lakes that they passed along the way. Chris sat stoically in the backseat, mind once again churning and unwilling to be drawn into mediocre conversation with the two adults in the front seat. Chris, even in insanity, had never really lost sight of his interests in hacking. Although he had passed through the eye of the storm and had been up close and personal with psychosis, not even the neuroleptics could touch his innate technological capabilities. So he sat in gloomy silence, deep in thought about future goals and the world that had previously been opened up to him. After several hours of travel, they reached their destination. They turned down familiar streets that Chris had not seen for several months. He watched the neighborhood as it unfolded before him, feeling somewhat like a prison convict who had finally secured a release from lockup and returned back home. They finally turned down their street. The day was still bright with an afternoon sun, and neighbors still busied themselves with mowing and gardening as Chris and family slowly turned into their driveway. Their arrival did not go without notice. They all slowly got out of the car, and neighbors who had been outside and seen the arrival of Chris and his family decided not to approach them. Consternation was evident in their faces. Chris was more an object of pity than one of the neighborhood kids. They reluctantly waved at the arriving family and then all hurried back into their homes to the safety of their lazy boys and television sets.

63. A Spirit World

ON A HOT AUGUST DAY, the teams at Grand Coulee wrapped up their studies. They had sent all manner of material through their own secure systems to their research centers, where it would be further analyzed by an assortment of technologists and scientists. They would spend an inordinate amount of time in this vein in order to set straight any of their own hypotheses and concerns as well as any risks and contingency plans if needed. Preston and his team saw the whole dramatic picture as fast as the camera lens panned the underwater fissure. In real time, they watched as the *Pegasus* sent up to them its testimony of a huge parallel crack that divided hard sediment like so many eggshells. They felt only a sense of foreboding and danger in what they had reviewed, and in their rather close and intimate circle there was a feeling of power. Theirs had been the first eyes to see what physical science had up its sleeve, and they were the first to encounter it firsthand.

August 10 had been decided upon as the day of departure. The day before was hot, but on the tenth, a wind started blowing in the early morning and buffeted the camp throughout the day. The men secured all their equipment. The change in weather was a little odd for a time of year generally draped in the unforgiving heat of the basin sun. The *Pegasus* had fared better; the truck that had brought here down to the lake had declined to make a return, so she had been piloted several miles downstream to a large, open, and flat area on private property in the evening hours. This had been done the preceding day, when the weather, although hot, was relatively calm. The farmer who had so generously opened up his land to them was paid handsomely, and the truck and small crane that would reload the sub easily made the trip to the water's edge and loaded the *Pegasus* back onto the lowboy, cloaked her in tarpaulin, and made their way back toward the small rural highways with pilot cars front and back. She once again was in transit, having unlocked the secrets of the Columbia.

Preston and his colleagues had not fared as well. As the day moved toward evening hours, great thunderheads moved over them. They had secured all the equipment and tied down that which could prove to be dangerous and injure some unsuspecting soul. The barometer dropped precipitously with the formation of the storm front, and by seven o'clock the men were all inside the assorted mobile units and campers that had served them as home and base of operations. The wind grew even fiercer. The first flash of lightning came at eight o'clock, quickly followed by thunderclaps and driving rain. Visibility was zero, and the entire camp became a shallow lake with rain still pouring down. At midnight the worst was over. Although they all needed a well-deserved rest, sleep did not come; instead they waited out the remainder of the storm and went outside to assess the damage.

The storm enshrouded the entire region, leaving some areas flooded. While it ravaged the Columbia and the foothills and cliffs, it also uncovered the spiritual dimensions of the area. As the men who had come to unlock her secrets took their cover on a ridge overlooking the entire expanse of lake and hills, a persistent and driving wind sent great flumes of dust and other flotsam hither and yon. Then, without warning, the rains came and revealed the remnants of an Indian burial ground, unassuming, long forgotten and untouched. It stood its post like a sentinel, looking down on the lake and dam below in silence. As the storm passed it revealed several more graves. A good dusting and scrubbing revealed eight sites in all, with only the moon above as captive audience to the uncovered spirit world below. Hours after the passing storm had moved to the west, a rock tumbled noiselessly from the top of one of the markers. It found its resting place in the stillness of the night. The storm had already passed.

64. Town

Mid-August was hot and unforgiving. Faint flumes of dust could be seen racing across the basin, only to add to the aggravation of area farmers and field laborers as they worked in the fields and attempted to harvest the beginnings of fall crops. Jake and Keith were no exception to the basin farmers, and like so many of them they had several acres of hay. They beat the hellish midday heat by starting early, knocking off at noon, and then restarting the operation in early evening for several hours. The routine was wearying and not without a monotonous undertone. It begged for at least one evening of relaxation and relief. The two brothers had made some inroads in spite of Chester's death: books started to look a little more balanced, and the bank was extending them a little more credit toward their crops. The machinery was holding together with the help of Keith's mechanic skills, and everything was running as smoothly as possible. The two men decided it was time for a night out.

The two men spent a productive Saturday swathing hay. Instead of knocking off with the heat, they found other work around the house to keep them busy. They finished up at six, returned to the house, and quickly fried up hamburger and potatoes and proceeded to clean up for the trip to town. There was almost ceremony to this endeavor; they each showered and shaved, slapped on aftershave, and searched for the cleanest pair of Levis and shirt, finishing up with a decent pair of cowboy boots and lastly the Stetson. When they finished, Jake called up Nora, who had a friend whom she felt would be perfect for Keith. With that, they left the house, jumped into the pickup, and made their way to town.

They drove the back roads into town, each with a beer and savoring the early evening air. Windows rolled down, they listened to killdeer scold their brethren and wing low over fields and sage. The brothers could smell the newly cut hay. All the sights, sounds, and smells of the evening only added to their sense of adventure. The trip to town was quick: they reached Royal City after about thirty minutes. There was still daylight, and the evening was warm and full of promise for lovers young and old. On their arrival they went straight over to Nora's. They ascended the outside stairs two at a time, reached the screen door, and rapped lightly in spite of the welcome chattering of the two females inside. Nora came quickly to the door and let the two dates inside.

Keith, who had gone along with apprehension on the promise of a blind date, was instantaneously gratified with Nora's matchmaking. She was a beauty in her late thirties with green eyes and red hair, and she seemed equally impressed with Keith. Nora quickly introduced her friend, Kathy, a local girl from Moses Lake, to Keith and Jake. They made small talk and then decided to walk into town to one of the local watering holes.

Saturday night in the summer was the busiest nights for the local bars. In Royal there were only a couple of these establishments, and the locals either went to one or the other depending on the entertainment available. Jake and company had no trouble in the decision and went to a nondescript joint complete with a couple of pool tables, dance floor, and jukebox. They made this decision without burdensome politics; it was the closest. The entourage went inside the Royal and secured a booth in a corner. It was still early enough to get a decent seat before the later arrivals of locals with a healthy thirst and a need to kick up their heels. They sat down unceremoniously and ordered up a pitcher of beer. With glasses filled, they toasted each other and then quickly engaged their dates into conversation and flirtation. Keith was batting a thousand with Kathy; after several minutes of lighthearted talk and ogling each other, they excused themselves and headed for the jukebox and a quiet moment of selecting songs and bonding. Jake and Nora dismissed them knowingly; they, too, wanted a quiet moment of gentle talk and cooing. During these brief minutes of adoration, Jake for some reason became increasingly aware of several men talking loudly at the bar. At first he paid little attention to these patrons, but after several minutes, their voices became louder, and this often meant a fight. Jake walked over to Keith and Kathy and brought them back to the table to keep a more watchful eye on the commotion at the bar.

Seated back at the table, Jake looked toward the center of activity. It was apparent that it was not an argument; this was something of a relief, as Jake and Keith had both had their fair share of barroom brawls in the past, and there was no need to cut a perfect evening short with broken noses and lost teeth. Jake and Keith both looked with interest toward the bar now. Jake made out several of his neighbors and townspeople, all of whom who appeared to be listening with keen interest to Bill Red Bones and Hoagland. Jake knew them both. Although he had little in common with the two men, he recognized them and soon found he was half eavesdropping on their conversation. He was only catching bits and pieces of what they were saying. Finally, with an all-consuming need to hear a little more of what was being said, he excused himself from the group, grabbed the empty pitcher, and proceeded toward the bar and the group of men. He hoped that his curiosity would not be obvious to his date and the others.

Jake quickly walked over to the bar and found a space next to Hoagland. Earlier, Hoagland had started the ball rolling on their trip down to Coulee with a couple of men who had already had too much to drink. The topic soon garnered enough interest that several more men ambled over to the source of excitement and listened raptly as Billy took over and talked of their recent excursion. Jake himself was listening with keen interest. Billy was retracing their stay as well as the comings and goings of the submarine and every aspect of their spying—at what, they could not quite fathom. Jake was oblivious to the refilled beer pitcher in front of him. He listened carefully as Billy relived the entire experience of watching clandestinely as the survey team positioned various antennae and instruments on the miniature sub and its two-man crew. Most importantly, there was mention of two men who on one of these excursions did not come back. This in itself was an ominous sign, not to mention the location of the site, close to Grand Coulee Dam.

Jake had heard enough. Initially his response was to dismiss what he had heard from the two men as so much cock and bull. He knew that the two men had a penchant for embellishing a story. Somehow, though, that did not seem to be the case here. If what they had revealed to the patrons at the bar was gossip, it was one of the finest stories that he had ever heard. Jake decided that even these two were incapable of creating such a yarn; they were too limited, and neither one of them had enough exposure to the technological world that they so convincingly spoke of. Jake grabbed the pitcher of beer and returned to the table. Without hesitation, the others asked him what had kept his interest at the bar. Jake mumbled a few words and told them that he would tell them later. The evening was still young, and he did not want to waste it with what he had heard at the bar.

The rest of the evening was spent with no mention of what Jake had heard at the bar. In fact, any mention of the subject was avoided at all costs. Nora and Keith both knew Jake well enough to understand that his reluctance to cover old ground was final, at least for now. The couples spent the rest of the evening dancing and enjoying each other's company. Keith and Kathy proved to be a great match, and at the end of the night, the two couples split up, Keith going with Kathy to her place and Jake taking Nora back to the farm. The night was all theirs.

Billy returned with Hoagland from town, and they parted ways, with Hoagland heading to the Basin. Billy returned to his superstitions, sensing that all was not right in the spirit world. As he had done numerous times before, he took up the ways of the medicine man. Outside, he lit a campfire and pulled out a small pouch with assorted animal bones and tossed them with great care into the dirt at his feet. He looked intently at the pattern with glaring fire casting its light on his face. He made a small shudder. The bones revealed a great catastrophe of water. They did not lie; his forefathers knew. In the early-morning hours, Billy gathered all his needs together and set out for the highest elevation he could reach above the Columbia. He would be saved from the ravages of the river with little time to spare.

65. The Conversation

Jake awoke early with Nora snuggled against him. He slowly shook off the remnants of the previous evening, got up, and splashed water on his face. He quietly went outside and began to think about what he had heard the previous evening. He had tried hard through the hours of conversation at the bar and the night's intimacy to shake the topic, but he had returned to it frequently. It seemed important, and even though he was often suspicious of gossip, this had a different flavor, almost ominous and thought-provoking. He heard Nora begin to stir. He watched her through the screen door as she slowly got out of bed. She stood in the early-morning sunlight, languishing in her beauty, and then moved slowly across the floor to the front porch, naked and searching for her lover. Jake and Nora met at the door, embraced, and once again returned to bed. It would be several hours before the two would get up and start the day.

Jake dropped Nora off at her apartment; he had directions to Kathy's and drove the half-mile or so over to pick up Keith. He found Keith sitting lazily on the front step, an easy smile on his face and a cup of coffee balanced on his knee. Kathy came out to greet Jake. She smiled in the shy abandon of a woman who had been fulfilled. She quietly kissed Keith, whispered to him, and then returned to the confines of her apartment. Keith nodded to Jake, and both men got in the Ford and headed back home.

Both men sat quietly the first several minutes of their trip back home, but it was a silence that would not last for long. Keith knew his brother all too well; there was something nagging on him, and he was aching to get it out. Keith watched the scenery as it raced by until halfway back to their ranch he finally asked Jake the question that begged to be revisited. He watched Jake carefully as his brother's face, often relaxed, took on a look of quiet desperation and concern. Jake finally spoke, conviction in his prose, and told Keith about the strange conversation that Billy Red Bones and Hoagland had relayed at the bar—the submarine, the two divers who did not seem to return, the many men, and the special equipment that they had watched over several days at Grand Coulee.

Having retold the story, Jake looked across at Keith, who now himself seemed puzzled and apprehensive by the gravity of what he had heard. He looked back at Jake and shrugged his shoulders. Both men felt a sense of despair and helplessness. They spent the rest of the ride in silence, both entrenched in private thought, attempting to fathom the future of their home and wondering whether catastrophe was in the cards. Both men knew that anything that happened upriver would either directly or indirectly affect them and their home; they were in harm's way.

66. Contingencies

Dave had been called in by his supervisor to attend a last-minute meeting. It was now late August, and he was unaware of the reason for the request. He still had been spending an inordinate amount of time attempting to capture the renegade virus that had caused so many problems earlier in the summer, and he felt that the meeting was somehow related to this. At eight o'clock, he arrived at the BPA building. The air was a little brisk, carrying an early sign of fall, but invigorating. His stride was quick as he entered into the inner sanctum of security, showed his credentials, and quickly entered a bank of elevators with several other men, all of whom ascended to the upper level with him. Dave stood quietly. The men who had gotten on the elevator with him were unfamiliar to him, which was odd. Most of the people he saw either getting on the elevators or milling about in the lobby were recognizable. The riders looked official and stoical; they uttered not a word to each other, and all seemed preoccupied. Dave felt a little out of place in their company but dismissed it as the usual claustrophobia that was always part of being cramped on board elevators. At the top floor, the men all got off and, along with Dave, headed straight for administrative offices. The furnishings were tasteful and well-appointed, and several paintings graced walls to either side as the party made progress toward their destination.

After seeing this part of the complex, Dave felt that management would be a nice way to wrap up his career. He intuitively followed the men into a large conference room where several important-looking individuals were either sitting or looking out the windows onto the panorama of Portland and the cascades to the north. The men were all ushered in with a gradual nodding of the head. Dave recognized that BPA's top management were all in attendance. He had never seen these men in person, only their photos in the monthly newsletters or memos that were sent out. It seemed odd to him that someone of his standing would be invited to such a high-level meeting as this. He had a feeling of confusion mixed with trepidation. He decided to keep his mouth shut unless for some reason he was called upon to give some bit of useful information.

Later arrivals came in after Dave and his cortege. They slowly began to fill the large room, but there seemed to be just enough seats at the large table to accommodate all of them. Dave scanned this crowd closely and recognized several key government officials in the mix. They were high-level officials, and he saw them infrequently on the news or giving interviews in local papers on some important topic. The men moved about uncomfortably in the room. Some went over to the buffet filled with coffee cups and helped themselves to the pastry. There was an uneasiness to all their actions, and Dave sensed that whatever was going to take place today would have great bearing not only on himself but others as well. He looked over to the person seated next to himself and excused himself to go to the bathroom. He needed a few minutes away from the intensity that he was already beginning to feel. The gentleman next to him excused him and indicated that he would hold his chair. Dave found the executive bathroom and quickly went to a stall, sat down, and began to methodically rub his temples, slowly and then in more vigorous motions, as if he could rub away the stress that he was encountering here—and the meeting had not even begun.

At first he didn't hear the two men who came in. They started talking about Grand Coulee Dam, unaware that there was a third party in attendance. Dave listened raptly as the two men discussed several issues that would be covered in that day's meeting. Although their speech was muted deliberately, they were close enough to the stall that Dave occupied to be overheard with ease. They left after several minutes, when the meeting was about to start.

Dave waited for the closing of the door behind them and quietly got up. Feeling a little nauseous, he went over to the sink and splashed water on his face feeling as if he were going to vomit. He knew what he had heard was just the beginning of what he would hear in the next hour or so, he regained his poise and returned to the others.

The top man of BPA took his place at the head of the table. He was flanked on either side by several directors and other high-ranking sundry officials. As Dave scanned the room, he noticed several men who looked out of place with all the executives. These men were dressed not in suits but in Levis and hiking boots and appeared unshaven. Later they were introduced as Kirk, a geology professor from CWU, and Preston, a lead diver. Dave felt that these two had some sort of significant role in the proceedings but couldn't quite put his finger on it. As for himself, he was still not sure what his role was in all this.

Without pretense, the BPA head opened with an acknowledgment to all the key players in attendance. His manner was stern and without humor, which Dave took as an omen of the topic that would be covered. He again looked at all the men in the room and watched their faces. Many were uneasy and pale, as if they had some knowledge of a great doom or event that would forever change their lives. Having overheard the conversation in the bathroom some ten minutes prior to the opening of the discussion, Dave himself could understand their apprehensions.

The speaker continued on in his soliloquy, scanning the room with each uninterrupted sentence to search for those who were confused or dissented from the views being laid out. He proceeded for several minutes, describing the progression of events from the late spring up until the present. He began with the grid problems, described the open spillways at Bonneville, and finally spoke about the several small earthquakes that had found their way inland to the Coulee region. Each on its own was rather insignificant, but together they made for compelling possibilities. He moved on, quickly, expertly, not to scare the audience but to let them digest what he had said, ruminate, and form their own opinions. At last he moved on to describe the impact of a waterway in chaos, discussing the collateral damage and possible loss of life. With that he looked beyond his audience, as if trying to see beyond a problem, and muttered about the need for contingencies. The men present in the room could identify the problem in all of its tangible qualities.

The BPA boss paused for several seconds and then turned to his next in command, who stood obediently and continued on with observations made using scale models of the Columbia River, its estuaries and dams, and the Hanford nuclear reservation. The Atomic Energy Commission officials listened carefully to their BPA counterparts; after all, they too shared the Columbia and its resources. Although their work was insulated from the outside world, they were not invulnerable to the wrath of a major waterway. The speaker explained in great detail how a scaled-down version of the entire grid of the Northwest was used, its volumes precise and computed into calculations that wavered only with the amount of rainfall. He made his point well, ending almost as abruptly as he had started. He paused and looked around the room for a familiar face. Then, seeing Kirk, he motioned for the professor to come to the podium. Kirk was then introduced to the audience.

Kirk grabbed either side of podium with sweating palms. He looked out over the sallow faces with consternation. He was unable to speak for several seconds until finally, after formulating his thoughts, he was able to approach the topic using his expertise and field work data. He briefly outlined the project, describing what he had hoped to accomplish and how the team had made its discoveries of the fissuring as well as the coincidental movement of quakes in the area. He described the repercussions of the quakes and finally narrated the underwater exploration of the several divers and the miniature submarine's findings. His brevity of manner was not lost on those in attendance, and to wrap up his speech he introduced Preston, who expanded on the geological findings of Kirk by describing the underwater anomalies, the hidden parallel rift that after so many thousands of years of dormant and static behavior had lengthened considerably with the physical movements out in the Pacific. The two men ended their joint efforts by rolling tape. All their efforts of the several days at the Coulee were summarized in their film, which showed first the ground findings of Kirk and his CWU team and then the foray across the river to denote physical changes in the topography opposite them. Finally, Preston and the diving team appeared to lend more credence to the division that went underwater. He told of the loss of two of his team members, whose bodies had not been recovered, and finally of the sub's findings. It was enough, and it was several minutes before those seated could finally vocalize their concerns and questions to the professionals involved.

Each government agency present already had its own contingency plan in place for such a catastrophe, but hearing of varying sides of the problem and its colossal possibilities only caused more alarm. They hadn't counted on anything of the scale that had been presented. Bureaucracies had been hampered by their own limited and clogged resources. They had to rely on outside contractors and consultants, who for the sake of corruption often muddied the picture. The representatives present all sat slack-jawed and in awe. They had no real answers to what they had heard—with the exception of one of the geologists, who in an effort at consoling them stated that the offshore quakes were limited in duration and it was quite possible that there would be no further activity in their lifetimes. Such an outcome would spare them all of the stress they were experiencing now, but what of the future?

The many officials listened as each man pushed forth his

own agency's agenda and concerns. All wanted a tangible report to take back to their departments. The meeting ended in late afternoon. It was a glum and concerned group of men who silently moved beyond the heavy, ornate doors of the BPA and padded down a heavy carpeted hallway to the bank of elevators, down to the mezzanine onto Portland streets, and finally to a good, stiff drink.

67. Hanford

THE OFFICIALS FROM THE HANFORD reservation returned home the following day. They, like many of their assorted counterparts, had left the meeting with a sense of fear. And like several of the officials who had been present at the BPA complex in Portland, they spent the night drinking at one of the local lounges until inebriation ushered them back to a downtown hotel where, upon arising and shaking off the previous night's hangover, they would make the trip back to Hanford and give their accounts of what they had heard. Only a few of the higher-echelon management made the trip. The return back to the tri cities was in silence. They followed the long, ribbon-like highway along the Columbia, more aware of its vastness than ever before. Each man had driven this particular highway several times before, and each had been guilty of looking at its natural beauty and the several dams upon the river benignly, never considering that even beauty could have potential rapturous possibilities. The three travelers made their way steadily upriver, traveling along the Oregon side, taking in the communities, the Bonneville Dam, and then finally the Dalles before crossing over the Maryhill Bridge and winding into the southeastern part of Washington, never once leaving sight of the river.

Their destination, several hours from Portland, was and is

well known, locked into isolation in the scrubby sagebrush lands that the Columbia had irrigated over the decades: Hanford. The vast repository for spent fuel rods had many secrets well out of the public eye, yet it lay on the banks of the Columbia and well in harm's way. The men returned to their clandestine base of operations, a place where only a highway passed by, and moved past the great government complex with all of its secrets and energy. Only the signature of blinking lights showed over desert skies to the car traveler. This was Hanford.

The three key players presented their concerns to a team of specialists and PhDs in the days to come. After several days of conferring with each other and the other government agencies, they would still feel overwhelmed with all their questions and impact studies. The issue was greater than all of them. Even the mighty Hanford was at risk, simply because of its need to be close to a source of water.

68. Old Ways

CHRIS LOST NO TIME IN returning to old ways and old routines. Summer was almost over, and he felt the need to get back to the keyboard that he had been denied so long. He continued to take his medicines as they were prescribed, generally with his parents' gentle insistence and oversight. His doctor recommended that his parents closely monitor his medication regimen, lest he forget to take the antipsychotics and once again fall into jeopardy. Chris acquiesced to the urgings of his parents and doctor and had a therapist who followed his progress on a twice-weekly basis. Trust was being built, and slowly his parents began to let Chris take the medications on his own. The therapist, after several weeks of hourly visits, began to wean Chris off the demanding visit pattern. After all, he maintained his stability, and at the rate he was going, the therapist felt that his patient could once again be independent.

Chris had impressed them all, but demons still lurked within him. In spite of all the medications that he was taking, he still had an unwritten agenda, and this he had not revealed to anyone. As the weeks progressed and he gained the trust and support of all who were involved in his return, he began to avoid taking some of the medications that had helped him. While his parents were at work or out of the house, he retrieved the computer and all the hardware that he had hidden so expertly. He set about reassembling it, his mind once again hungering for his world of chaos and hacking. His parents felt that his forays behind the screen were innocent; they were not concerned when the computer reappeared back at its former site. They had never quite understood what Chris was capable of, and they had not suspected his destruction of it before his break, trusting that his putting it away was just a small part of his paranoia. Essentially, they brushed it off.

Chris was meticulous in his efforts. He spent most of his time at home, and when his parents asked why he didn't try to reconnect with his friends, he would shrug them off. His parents chose not to pursue that argument. Well into the fourth week at home, Chris began to skip the Clozaril. Its side effects were overwhelming, and he felt that he was losing his edge to the tiny yellow pills. He knew that he would have to be careful with stopping such a potent medication; after all, it was determined to be a last resort for Chris's case, and it also required lab work to monitor his WBCs. Chris slowly began to wean himself off. He was cunning in his work, substituting the Clozaril with a holistic concoction that he had bought at a health food store. His parents were unsuspecting; he had gathered them in his trust, and they were none the wiser. So the charade was in full swing by October. Chris was off the Clozaril completely, taking a thrice-daily dose of vitamins in lieu of his antipsychotic medication.

Slowly, he was once again entering into the world of paranoia and hallucination. Chris was skilled at disguising his regained psychosis; he was charismatic enough to continue with fooling his parents, and through the day he spent little time at the house but would take long walks in order to let the inner voices speak to him, giving their commands to a committed accomplice. Chris once again became entrenched in the computer. As his family slept, he once again began hacking, breaking into new sites and retracing his steps back to the old. One of these was the BPA.

69. Old Demons Return

DAVE WAS WELL INTO HIS divorce proceedings and, with custody issues always in the foreground, again buried himself in his work. It was almost like a stress reliever. With the current concerns with the fragility of the Columbia and its breeches, there was more than enough on his plate to keep him busy for some time to come. He was frequently arriving at work much earlier than his colleagues, working on either one plan or the other; he was becoming quite dedicated in his efforts of finding alternatives to the grim picture that had been presented at the BPA meeting. He attacked his work in earnest, hoping to find a resolution to the complicated picture and all its possibilities. He continued his strict routine well into October, working late and sometimes returning to the office on Saturdays and Sundays to search through unending materials and software. He labored at a maddening pace, seeking the demons that had plagued his system in the past. On a quiet Tuesday evening well after the rest of the staff had gone home, Dave found himself staring intently at his screen, half-groggy from the continuous hours that he had spent behind his screen. He shook his head violently in order to shake the cobwebs from his brain. He thought what he was now looking at was some sort of a mirage, but slowly the nondescript anomaly began to take form, revealing its intent with a bizarre message. The hacker had returned, and with the presence came a fusillade of technological flim-flam that Dave had already seen. He stayed at his station and watched the screen to see what developments would arise. What he saw was innocent enough, but the message was also insidious, encouraging the reader to open up the package, unleashing the monster and all its dubious features.

Dave avoided this. Instead he took several notes, made a few important phone calls to upper management, and then bunked out in one of the offices until he could start out fresh in the morning. He slept fitfully. The small cot was less accommodating than his bed at home: it was hard, and one good roll would have placed him squarely on the floor. He made a sincere effort to get some sleep in spite of the lack of comfort, but as the hours ticked toward early morning, he decided to get up and wash up. He had managed to find a shower in one of the executive's offices. He went ahead and used it, and after drying off and dressing he went to a small kitchen, made a quick cup of tea, and then returned to his computer screen.

His office was quiet. He looked out the large office windows and could see Portland. The city was still asleep; the dim, gray light of a rising sun was beginning to cast its early-morning glow over a city that would slowly wake to the start of a new day. Dave sipped at the tea, lost in his thoughts, and then walked back to the computer and made various entries into the memory. He would continue throughout the day. He was once again facing his old nemesis, and now it seemed there were a few new tricks up the sleeve of whoever was hacking into their system.

Dave spent the next several days trying to establish the origins of the virus. He enlisted several of his colleagues, who programmed with him in this vein. The days went by quickly, and although the virus was irritating to all who encountered it, it was still benign. It did not unleash itself or create havoc as it had months before, but it was insidious, creeping into various information banks and staying. It did so, though, without altering or destroying current memory, Dave kept up his frenetic search until he had spent almost a week playing cat and mouse with the enigma in his screen. Then he decided to sign off and let some of his colleagues take over. He knew that he needed a couple of days to back off; he was losing his objectivity, and there were others equally capable of resuming this technological battle. He made arrangements to take a few days off and decided to spend his brief hiatus in White Salmon, at a bed and breakfast with a magnificent view of the Columbia and reasonable rates. He would also take along a laptop; the bed and breakfast was set up for the Internet, so he would always be in constant communication with the office. He needed the break and knew that whatever happened in the following days, he would be in the loop.

70. The *Echo*

October skies floated lazily overhead as the *Echo*, a fifty-foot research ship, sat quietly in calm seas. It was now early evening. The fifteen men who made up her crew were a menagerie of PhDs and seagoing salts. The specialists on board consisted of geologists, mineralogists, and a volcanologist studying the faults off the coast. His agenda was simple: to correlate the material with past volcanic activity, giving the academic world some grist for their mills as well as exploring the potential of future eruptions. Each man had his own agenda. Close quarters often made tempers raw, but the men had managed to stay out of each other's way. The crew was the captain, a navigator, the mate, and assorted deckhands, all experienced with the open sea and its behavior changes. The ship was well equipped with the latest sonar and a plethora of other gadgets and gizmos that challenged the crew in the tightness of quarters. Technicians took care of the guts of the operations at sea, and lastly there was a doctor on board for emergencies. They sat a good hundred miles off the Washington coast.

Some of the crew had just finished dinner. They would eventually rotate back to one station or the other and relieve the next man for his meal break. The ship had been out to sea since early April and had already been involved with identifying a previous movement in the Pacific fault. Either there were days and weeks of boredom or, as with the event in June, a heightened sense of apprehension and awareness. The crew did not expect any more activity on the Pacific shelf. They enjoyed the camaraderie that each man brought to the plate, and several went topside to watch the setting sun in a red, benevolent sky and have a quick smoke before either returning to their stations or relaxing in the confinement of their bunks to read before turning in. This was the routine the men had established over the several months that they had been together: research with a little recreation thrown in to counter the vagaries of professional agendas.

The vessel moved noiselessly northwest at fourteen knots through the calm seas. Two-thirds of the crew was now fast asleep in the bunks below. On the bridge the captain watched the instrumentation scrupulously. His navigator had pointed out an anomaly on the radar which now seemed to be more obvious, and they both took careful note of the time: 12:01 a.m., a new day. The vessel rolled slightly back and forth, not violently but noticeably enough to wake up some of the lighter sleepers. Within minutes the boat rolled again. This time it succeeded in waking up the remainder of the crew. The instrumentation throughout the ship was blinking and alarming. The captain looked out the dappled window toward the horizon and felt that the ship was listing; he righted his course until once again they sat quietly, with only the gentle waves rolling against her keel. A geologist had managed to get some readings from one of the many oscilloscopes and checked the readings of the various printouts. High-frequency sonograms were now feeding information through their on-board computers. Printers began emitting reams of information, which the specialists quickly absorbed. Each man grabbed a piece of whatever printout looked most interesting.

In the meantime, the boat was steadier. The waves that had lashed out so violently earlier were now incorporated back into calmer seas. But below them, and unknown to them, the calamity of the Pacific plates was once more in its physical tango. The plates had moved violently, sliding one over the other, and it was this movement that had caused the *Echo* its brief interlude with a violent sea. The geologists began to examine what had been experienced on board, suspecting a repeat of the fault movement. They spent several minutes interpreting the radar imaging as well as the other electronic data on board with some consternation. Minutes after the episode, their satellite link with land began to reveal even more details of the event. The Golden, Colorado, team had centered an earthquake toward the eastern end of Washington but had also found movement near where the *Echo* was now steaming. Officials inland were now requesting any added evidence of this through their link-ups, and there was a priority to the request. The well-diversified team of professionals and crew spent several more hours gathering further information on the plate movement. They sent this to the various agencies that had requested the material, and although it was sent rapid-fire, the real calamity was one that they themselves would not be part of. They were safe at sea, out of harm's way.

71. Golden

Golden slept under the big Colorado skies, the town outstretched and reaching toward the Rockies and beyond. It was frontiersy and outspoken, with famous neighbors including Coors as well as the USGS with its National Earthquake Information Center. The site was well chosen; it was connected to the 2,500 seismograph stations throughout the United States, including Alaska and Hawaii. In the event of any anomaly, these independents all fed into RSNs, which would provide real-time advisories and monitoring as an event unfolded. Golden now sat serenely under a fall sky and beside the Rockies, formidable and monolithic, far removed from many of the calamities that had rained terror around the world with the first hint of tremors. The USGS felt safe at Golden in monitoring the seismic rumblings.

The town slept as evening hours crept toward the morning. The men inside the USGS watched monitors for any nuance that could predict seismic activity. Recently the Washington coast had been of interest, and although they were not concerned this evening, the men who worked this late hour always had concerns of history repeating itself. They had seen activity in 1999 around Mt. Hood and Mt. St. Helens as well as out in the Strait of Juan De Fuca. They reminded themselves that the tectonics liked to move when you least expected it, much of the time in a part of the world that was still sleeping soundly. Several men had gathered outside in the brisk, late-night fall air to catch a smoke and chat. The time was 11:50 p.m. Now caught up in the camaraderie of smoking and gossip, they did not hear the first demands from one of their colleagues to return instantly. The command came again, breaking the group up. All returned inside to the first networking and interfacing of a quake which was now registering off the coast of Washington with a 5.5 on the Richter scale. The time was exactly 12:01 a.m. in the Pacific time zone. A cascade of events began to occur as the plate made its movements known. Seismometers from several hundred to thousands of miles away denoted the real-time event as well as the seismic wave form. All this information was being provided to the USNSN, to forward on to the communities that would possibly be affected by the quake. She began innocently enough, way off the coast and several miles down under the ocean floor, but she had more death in her than innocence. As the seismic activity was closely watched, she began to send her calling cards: P and S waves that snaked their way to the east well beyond the Cascade Range, toward the Columbia and Grant County. In Golden, the many specialists followed the quake's activity with consternation. They had watched the dynamics to a smaller degree earlier in the summer, and they looked on helplessly as once again the quake's fingers poked at the terrain in the basin, revealing an even larger crack in the fragile landscape. The quake had movement. The alert went out; it liked to return to old haunts.

72. Interface

CHRIS HAD BEEN SLEEPING IN till late afternoon. Today he woke up at approximately four o'clock in the afternoon. He checked his clock twice to see if he was reading the time wrong and then hastily got out of his bed. He headed for the shower and spent the next forty-five minutes attempting to return to a wakeful state. He finished in time to hear his mother return home from work. She had been accustomed to his nocturnal routines, sleeping late and up most of the night. She refused to see the face of insanity returning. Rather, she thought that Chris had some meaningful employment via the Internet that kept him busy most of the night. As far as his behavior, she felt that there was no great change; he was still the nerdy kid that he had always been, only a little older. Chris's dad had been away for several days, so he was unaware of the current status in the household. Although he had called several times a week, Chris's mother had failed to give any hint over the phone of Chris's behavior. She felt that it was of no concern and that it would eventually pass. So mother and son kept up the pretense. Chris was still adept at presenting himself as a sane member of the household, and his mother was perfectly happy to throw objectivity out the window.

Chris ate dinner with his mother. Conversation was brief and without any focus, basically mundane and trivial. The rest of the evening progressed on that note. They watched TV for several hours after dinner until the eleven o'clock news came on. Chris watched his mother retire to her room. He told her he was going to stay up a little longer, and after several minutes he turned off lights and television and went to his room. Down the hallway and through a partially opened door, he listened for the sounds that he knew would give him the all-clear to enter into his Internet world. He heard the gentle snoring of his mother, who was now deep in her own slumber. Chris proceeded. Several weeks had passed since his incarceration at the hospital, but that did not prevent him from keeping touch with a select few who were now part of his inner sanctum, including one in particular with whom he had interfaced on several recent hackings in an attempt to once again throw the government and its assorted agencies into turmoil. It was with this conspirator that Chris had reentered the BPA and its vanguards to once again place a virus. The partner in crime provided a feint in the illicit movements put through the BPA's power grid, a decoy, while the real work was being done on a specific time frame. Even with the system down, the clock was ticking.

Tonight was the night; Chris had communicated this to Matt via the mail, safe because it was certified free from bugging or capturing of signals. The specifics were given in great detail.

They were to key in at approximately 11:55 p.m., wait five minutes, and then set the plan in motion. At midnight, with the help of a few insidious helpers in the BPA's network of computers, the hibernating virus would spring to life. It did not disappoint them. At the midnight hour, both young men watched their screens with keen interest. A cascade of events unfolded at that precise time, and slowly up and down the entire power grid of the Columbia river, each and every dam from the Bonneville to Grand Coulee slowly and deliberately swung open all its spillway gates, letting forth the foaming and raging torrents of water behind its cement walls. Chris knew nothing of the added aspect to his plan. He felt a brief shaking while in the throes of his excitement, looked around his room, and saw some movement of personal items and bric-a-brac. He concluded that it was a minor earthquake. The time was now 12:01 a.m.

73. Chaos

AN EERIE WIND BLEW HIGH above the Grand Coulee. A native burial ground was now experiencing the first movement of the earthquake. One of the more elaborate burial sites, which had several rocks piled high, was now swaying back and forth. This continued for several minutes until all the stones had independently rolled off the site and into oblivion. The spirits had awakened from their deep sleep. Below, the river seemed to rise. The cliff walls swayed rhythmically, and whole chunks of rock fell off in response to the quake. Finally, the deep crevice that had formed from the earlier quakes came alive once more. Under the great dam, a momentum was building. The fissure that had been under the close scrutiny of the geological team only weeks earlier was answering to the ravages of the physical world. A calamity of grinding and groaning, which now became more intense, was turning the age-old bedrock to which the dam anchored itself into liquid, a flowing river of rock that was incapable of stopping the breeching of the dam. The crack widened quickly as the movement of its fingers pushed and pulled at the weakest points. It traveled quickly, wedge-like and powerful. Externally and without warning, the eleven spillways now rolled back in quiet obedience to some unseen command. The lake responded by sending its confluence over the sides of the dam to the riverbed below. The time was now 12:05 a.m.

Within the viscera of the grand structure, pressures began to reveal themselves to the men inside. First the control rooms, with their assorted gauges and monitoring devices, came alive, independently responding to the movement of the fissure beneath the dam. The huge Westinghouse turbines lost their monotonous hum; instead there was a strange ebb, then moments of silence as once again they tried to resume their connection to the power grid. This lasted for moments, until the force of the quake and the volume of water behind the dam began to work its way into the many cracks that revealed themselves throughout the structure. The added flow of water now going over the spillway only accelerated the inevitable. The dam was losing her powerful footing on the trillions of gallons of water behind her.

The teams of men who labored inside of her had no time. The water quickly filled her chambers, seeking its level and the beyond. There were no alternatives and no heroes, only a monolith giving way to nature's forces and bringing a watery world to the men inside her.

74. Electric City

Few stirred at this early hour. A few locals at one of the town taverns with a view of the dam watched as the artificial lighting played over its surface. Without warning, the patrons felt movement under their chairs. Outside they could see a swaying, and then the great spillways opened and released their confluence. After the movement had stopped, the lighting revealed several cracks toward the base of the dam and up its sides. Water began to gush out of these, revealing larger flaws, until great volumes of unabated torrents poured forth. The men and women inside the bar sobered; they sensed the inevitable. Hurriedly they ran outside to parked cars, fearing the unknown. Most, in a manic state, had great difficulty with the easy task of turning over the ignition. Fraught with terror, the ones who were able to start their cars made a hurried effort to head for high ground. The lake halted their journeys, swallowed them up, and without great fanfare began its journey to the south unimpeded by any natural or manmade barricade. It now was on the move.

75. Stirrings

Ned could not have visualized in his wildest dreams the events that would occur on this mild, wet October evening. He had spent many of his carefree hours down at the lake in various interests, often just to escape the mundane demands of his lodgers. Much of the season had been nasty, raining often, keeping many of the tourists inside and out of the damp. The lake was higher than usual. In the past, rain had been scarce during the summer months, but this year, the weather was unusual. The lake was at capacity, aided by heavy snowfalls in the Cascades. Ned had feared at one point that his cabins would be in danger of flooding, but the lap of the water never quite made it up to the cottages. Ned now sat in the solitude of his kitchen. The day had been odd: the lake was extremely still, and the waterfowl that he was so accustomed to hearing as they flew precariously across the water's surface seeking out prey were absent. There had been a deep stillness all day; even the gentle rain seemed to have fallen silently. Ned concluded nothing from this. He shrugged it off to the weather, but in his gut he was apprehensive.

Ned turned in at nine. Several hours later he was still wide awake. He felt a shudder traveling through his entire body. Plates rattled, and the cottage seemed to take on a brief life of its own. This continued for several minutes until once again he was stable. Checking the clock, he saw that it was now midnight. Ned, having survived the initial shock of the quake, chose to lie still in his bed, lest he be struck down by a demon without warning. He made no attempt to leave the safety of his bed for more than an hour until his curiosity was piqued by several strange noises that he was now hearing from the outside. The noise was almost deafening and remarkably sounded somewhat like a waterfall.

With his heart beating loudly in his chest, he quickly pulled on his pants and boots, threw on his jacket, grabbed a lantern, and went outside. He was not alone: his tenants also were watching the phenomena. They had looks of astonishment on their faces and were being soaked by the fine mist of the turbulent waters. For the next several hours, Ned and his patrons watched as the great lake began its conquest to find a new level. Billions, maybe trillions, of gallons of water was now racing by them.

Ned watched well into morning. The ravages of the water were impressive; he knew that well below them, the full extent of the flood was taking place. He only ventured a guess and then said a brief prayer. Looking back at the shoreline, he could see that the water's edge was retreating several feet an hour. There was nothing to do but hope.

76. The Airstream

Jake, Nora, and Keith had spent a quiet evening at the farm. The work was now slowing down with the advent of fall, a time for rest, rejuvenation, and repairing ailing machinery that had been overlooked during the busier times of summer. Tonight the three sat and discussed what the future might hold. Jake now talked about marriage, which Nora had heard before but never really given much thought. Tonight Jake seemed more sincere. Then there was silence, as if deep thought were required when talking about matrimony. The topic changed. Once again, they talked about the finances and keeping their debts down. The weather had been wet, and this had a major impact on their harvest. As always, the brothers were optimists and decided they would do better the following year. The three then went outside, sat down on the porch, and lit their cigarettes. They watched the rain as it formed tiny puddles in the driveway and listened to its resonant pitter-patter on the roof of the porch. Even with the rain, there was a deep silence. Not even the sound of cars could be heard as they traveled down the highway along the Columbia. They each commented on this, that they were unaccustomed to the lack of any outside noise. It was almost deafening, like a void that was not filled. The night was bizarre. Even the farm animals were quiet, bedding down earlier in the evening as if they were aware of some ominous event and deduced that it would be better to sleep through it. The three on the porch finished their cigarettes and decided to go to bed. Keith went inside while Jake and Nora opted for the trailer, a habit they had established months ago while in the infancy of their relationship.

The trailer had served them well, giving them isolation and serving their needs for intimacy without distraction or the fear of waking others with their early-morning lovemaking. They entered the trailer, quickly stripped, and were in each other's arms. They slept for what seemed to be only several minutes before they were awakened by a thundering noise, like several freight trains approaching from the north. Jake attempted to get out of bed while Nora remained motionless, overwhelmed with fear. In the next several minutes they were thrown about in the trailer as it was broken from its moorings. There was no way of peering outside, as the windows had long ago been fitted with coverings and welded shut, with the exception of one very small window that provide some scenic value as well as air. The Airstream was now moving rapidly; at the same time, they were being tossed up and down violently. The flood waters had progressed quickly and already had leveled everything in their path. Their appetite was growing.

Jake and Nora were helpless; they tried to hold on to each other as the trailer was being tossed about on waves twenty feet and higher. They were lucky, however; the Airstream was durable and remained intact in spite of the pounding it was getting from the rapturous waters. The couple was propelled down the Columbia, unable to see the destruction and death in their wake. In the waters were everything from homes to cars, livestock, and all the flotsam and jetsam that would follow in the wake of the flood. Behind them the damage was done, and what lay in front was the continuation of the flood as it would gain even more strength in its inevitable journey toward the mouth of the Columbia.

It was now three o'clock. They were completely thrashed about, covered with all manner of trauma, including bloody noses and abrasions as well as several deep cuts. Luckily they had no broken bones, but with the repeated trauma they did not know how long they would last out the pummeling. The river held them tight for several miles until by chance the Airstream broke free of the main current and moved toward the periphery of the flood. They began to go around a rocky outcropping that had not been submerged by the flooding. As they continued their course, the silver trailer took the pummeling of the waters. Great waves formed around its silver shell.

Its passage stopped at the outcropping. An errant wave tossed the projectile up into the air, onto the rocks that had managed to not be submerged by the flood. It now sat wedged a good twenty feet above the main volume of water, its rounded silvery nose facing almost straight up. The flood continued its progress unabated well below them.

Jake and Nora had the bare minimum in survival essentials. Each held on to the other for warmth. The trailer had been able to withstand the torrents without breaking up, and the couple dried off with one of several blankets that had been stored for hunting trips. They also had bottled water and canned food. The main discomfort now came from the angle of their berth, uncomfortable but tolerable. They would stay in the confines of the trailer for several days. Periods of shock and fear would keep them united. Outside was a world that they could not see from the relative safety of the Airstream.

Hours, then days elapsed as the ravages of the failing dams took their toll. Whole towns and cities passed by the trailer, leaving their remnants behind. Homes, vehicles, livestock, and corpse upon corpse bobbed up and down as the flood carried its bounty on toward the Pacific. What was left was total destruction. Towns that had once lined the Columbia all washed away. Wenatchee, the largest of these, sat under several feet of water, its loss in the tens of thousands of souls, and the flood had yet to make its most significant claims. Several days passed before the roiling waters began to become calm once again. Jake and Nora, still cuddled to each other, listened intently for some sign, any sign, that the disaster was ebbing and that search parties were looking for survivors.

On their fourth day they were rewarded. The turmoil outside had seemed to let up; they noticed a new calm. The water rushing outside was more placid now; gone was the deafening roar of the flood at its zenith. They had survived the onslaught in the Airstream. Its hulking silver skeleton withstood the test, wedged tightly in the rocky outcroppings that elevated it from the rushing waters below. Outside came the gentle whap, whapping of a helicopter, at first far off. It flew low, fifty feet above the water, its crew scanning the waters and the horizon for any survivors. Below them bodies bobbed lazily, some floating into each other. Livestock with feet pointing up also shared the waters, and the odor of decay pervaded. The crew held rags to their faces as they continued up the Columbia. As the helicopter got closer to the Airstream, they could see a hand reaching through an opening. The pilot alerted other crew members. The copter, with all its immense bulk, now levitated effortlessly as a man began to push back what was a door and revealed two people inside. Within minutes the helicopter sent down a basket for the two survivors and in rapid succession brought both up to safety.

On board, Jake and Nora thanked their saviors. Then they began to look back at what they had not been able to see from within the bowels of the trailer. They began to see the full range of what they had lived through. Protected from the wrath of the flooding river while inside the trailer, they could not have imagined what was happening outside. Now, inside the helicopter and able to look at the waters below, they could see the remnants of death: the floating carcasses, human and animal, and all else that had been carried away from its home by the marauding flood. The helicopter crew continued on with their passengers, searching for those lucky enough to have found some safe haven, but came up empty handed. Running low on fuel, they quickly altered their direction and headed back to their base camp. They would drop off their two passengers, where they would be treated and allowed to rest and ponder the results of all that had happened to them.

77. White Salmon

DAVE WOKE WITH THE FIRST signs of trouble, several loud sirens blasting for what seemed to be an eternity. It was three o'clock in the morning, and he was still in a dream state, although the sirens had most certainly given him a jolt. Outside was a deathly silence, broken only by the shrillness of the sirens. Minutes passed, and without hesitation Dave was getting dressed. He looked outside his window. Lights were coming on up and down the street, and several people were outside, either in small huddles or running in and out of their homes. The sirens continued with their lonely wail, and as Dave hurried down to the meeting area of the bed and breakfast, he could see that he was not alone. All the lodgers were assembled in the common area, some with pajamas on and others in various states of dress. No matter—there was no concern for the proper attire at this moment. Outside came a series of obnoxious knocks and bell ringing. The owner quickly answered the door and was met by an official-looking young man who introduced himself as a police officer. Quickly he stated his business and exited into the dark. The owner now came into the large living room and, with a look of fear on his face, told all of his guests that soon they would either have to leave or take their chances of being flooded.

He painted a grim picture. Grand Coulee had breached, and the domino effect went into play. A string of dams downriver from her could not stop the volume of water; each dam had fallen like a house of cards. The audience was somber with the news.

The owner continued in his soliloquy. He pointed out that White Salmon had an elevation advantage. It was on relatively high ground as compared to the many towns and cities that were being decimated by the surging waters. He gave them a 50-percent chance that the flood might miss them. Dave decided that the odds were in their favor and would ride it out or perish.

The guests decided that they too would take their chances. After all, their sites of egress were all but eliminated. Already, panic was taking place outside, and the roads were beginning to become clogged with the families who thought that the only option was to try to outrun the devastation heading toward them. In the end there would be several wrecks and fistfights as a result of the mayhem. The sirens continued their wail, and the patrons of the bed and breakfast now busied themselves, working for their own survival. Under the direction of the owner, they began to eliminate the assorted risks. They shuttered windows, checked all the doors, and placed loose items down in the basement. This kept all of them busy for a good hour. Now and then they listened to the radio to monitor the progress of the descending hell.

Hell made its entrance with stealth. In their industry of preparation, the tenants were oblivious to the outside noise or lack of it. Instead they continued in their movements. Outside there was complete silence. It was now nearing five in the morning, and without warning the billions of gallons of water that had been locked behind the many dams now coursed violently below them. All of those inside the hotel felt the first shock moments before the flood approached. The impact of the flood made itself known by violently shaking the house and all its contents. Those inside found themselves helpless and without equilibrium. They grabbed on to each other in a last-ditch effort to remain standing. This was futile. Items that had not been placed out of harm's way found their way to the floor as the house continued its rocking and swaying motion.

Each of the tenants now said his own private prayer. They were completely humbled by the event that was occurring outside their door. Death itself was a mere twenty feet below them, and in the gorge the leviathan took its victims without remorse. Biggs

Junction, The Dalles, and any community that had hugged the Columbia shoreline now succumbed to the ensuing flood.

Several hours elapsed. The bed and breakfast held to its small piece of real estate, its guests ensconced inside. The waters continued in their race to the Pacific, but their level was just below the foundation of the house. It was enough of a margin for the survival of Dave and all the others who now occupied the house with him. There would be no relief for several days, but they got their first real glimpse of the destruction a day after the initial flooding began. Outside they saw the remnants of entire cities and towns floating by on muddy waves. With the flotsam and jetsam were also the remains of those who had perished with no chance to flee. They now made the journey downstream lifeless and waxen, bloated and mannequin-like, with nothing to denote their lives other than the smell of death that now permeated the air.

A week passed. The Columbia continued its rampage, but now it moved more softly. It had found its level over a period of several days, which had made it possible for Dave and his fellow survivors to survive the flood, a mere ten feet from the cresting. It would be days later that all of them would fully realize the enormity of their luck. Dave and the entourage were helpless against all that had transpired outside the relative security of the bed and breakfast. They had listened to the full scope of the flood, and in the days that followed they were able to snatch an occasional glimpse of the horrific scenery that flowed effortlessly by them. They decided among themselves that they would take turns listening and watching for the first signs of rescue. Outside they could hear the monotone whap-whap of helicopters that busied themselves going up and down the river, picking up anyone who was lucky enough to have survived. They knew that it was a matter of days before they too would be picked up.

That day came one week after the flood began. A crew of four men flying in a Huey saw a frantic waving from the hotel. They hovered for several minutes a good hundred feet above ground, but with their binoculars they easily could see the anxious faces as they began to appear in various locations of the house and on the porch. Several men had ventured out and now waved wildly lest the copter, for some odd reason, should not site them.

Rescue began within minutes. The helicopter's pilot expertly maneuvered the big bird to a point several feet above the house. Two of the men inside the helicopter rigged the winch with safety harness and sent the cable with harness down toward the weary survivors. The women were first to be brought aboard. One by one they found themselves twisting helplessly as the cable lurched them toward the open mouth of the helicopter and into the lap of safety. On board each was directed toward a location out of harm's way. The crew took on seven passengers. Satisfied with their manifest, the pilot gave a nod, and a crew member yelled at the men below that they would return. The helicopter made its ascent and soon was only a speck in the southern skies.

Several hours later, Dave and the other men would again hear the rotating blades of the helicopter, its powerful gyrations getting closer until again it hovered above the house and plucked the remainder of the ragged inhabitants into the open bowels of the Huey for one more trip to its base on the Oregon side of the Columbia. Dave caught one last glimpse of the destruction as they started their incline. All below him had been claimed by the Columbia in its fury. He felt safe now, no longer in harm's way as he flew far above the lifeless forms that now littered the entire width and breadth of the river below. Dave and his fellow survivors now sat quietly. No man spoke; they didn't have to.

78. Epilogue

The river eventually became docile several days after the initial flooding. Now its course was unabated, its current was stronger, and the concrete breeches that for so long had supervised its flow and navigation stood without authority. The monolithic structures that had once performed their duties of altering a great river's currents were destroyed. Here and there at various sites on the river, great pieces of concrete littered the shoreline. The thousand-ton concrete rocks had been the great gates that held back the volumes of river that begged to push on and empty into the Pacific. Portions of each dam managed to survive the onslaught; whole walls of aggregate sat totem-like, 150 feet tall, like some unnatural physical anomaly still with a foothold in the bedrock of the river. Water flowing by effortlessly and silently bore testament to the great catastrophe that had redefined their nature. Grand Coulee sat eerily. A large, gaping hole now defined the portion of the dam where several of its spillways had once been. Half of the dam was gone, much of it washed several miles downstream with the first quake. At its lowest point, its underbelly too had been breached, forming a large crack that ran horizontally along the width of the dam, leaving much of the structure teetering precariously until chunks would fall free into the already-littered river.

The flood destroyed all in its path, its last stop Portland. Although the inhabitants had warning enough, the highways soon became clogged with the panic-stricken. The water eventually would flood much of Portland and in its quest leave several thousand more drowned or missing. The picture was still incomplete: with the loss of all the hydroelectric power that was generated by all of the dams, the entire Northwest had been catapulted back into the early 1900s. The giants of technology failed; Microsoft, Boeing, and all the fledglings of the tech industries were silenced. A domino effect was in play as all the investors of the great marketplace of the world were affected by the Columbia. And so the parable would continue.

How strange that one river could play such an important role in a country's welfare. Beyond the marketplace, the count of lives lost increased daily. Epidemics of cholera and all the other diseases associated with it would increase the already mounting death tolls. No avenue of recourse would be left unturned, as health agencies would all be involved in the epidemics that came after the flood. Where communities and cities had once existed on the shores of the river now stood wastelands. Only remnants were left: pieces of highways, bridges, and the concrete buildings that had held tight as the great volumes of water had washed over them, taking the path of least resistance, robbing from these monolithic structures and rendering them useless hulks of their former dignity, leaving nothing behind. The ruination was not complete. No stone left unturned.

The flood had also leveled Hanford, its reactors devastated by the tsunami that had passed over it. The radioactive fuel rods that had been sent to Hanford for burial deep in the labyrinth of underground tunnels and storage cells had also been exposed. The chambers were not resistant to the physical forces of billions and trillions of gallons of water pushing into even the most minute of cracks and crevices. Hanford gave up its progeny with reluctance; the containers that had held tightly to their secrets for so long managed to keep their deadly contents safely encapsulated, sparing the great river from further insult. The containers would bob about in the river for several weeks while the nuclear industry went about recapturing them and transferring them to other facilities that could handle the deadly ingredients. After several weeks, even the flow of the raw sewage was no longer a threat. The river cleansed itself, washing the raw effluent out into the Pacific. The Columbia was now complete again. Unhindered and majestic, she was supreme, her course unaltered by the hand of man.

JAKE AND NORA WOULD EVENTUALLY return to what was left of Schawana. Several months passed before it was safe for return. Their high hopes of finding any vestige of the farm so that they could start rebuilding and rekindling their dreams were all over. The journey back dashed these premature hopes within the first ten miles of the rebuilt road that they traveled on their return. There highway paralleled the remainder of Highway 10; bits and pieces remained, but little else. The surveyors had followed its path and piece together a temporary roadbed along the Columbia in order to reestablish connection to old town sites. It was on this graveled and pitted road that Jake and Nora would travel to their destination in a four-wheel-drive F150. The only thing that was more discouraging was the actual ride in the beat-up Ford cab.

The farm was completely gone, as was everything that could even remotely be identified with it: outbuildings, barn, and farm machinery were all wiped from the face of the earth. Most important was the human loss. Keith was also gone, and his body was never found. Jake had been grieving all along, but before their return he had some glimmer of hope that a miracle would happen, that Keith would meet them as they drove toward the house. He looked around toward the opposing cliffs and started to cry inconsolably. Nora held him close and said nothing. Later in the day they would leave, no longer feeling the ties that had made the place home.

Driving up the precipitous path toward a new future, they caught a glimpse of the Airstream. It winked at them with a silvery eye, held steadfast against all that nature had dished out, and seemed quite at home wedged tightly between the rocks that had saved their lives. They looked at each other with a brief smile and kept on driving, slowing only to take one last glance at the battered, bullet-shaped shell that had saved their lives.

Dave would return to the river. He now had a new base of operations farther inland. He was also one of the few lucky survivors able to reunite with his family. After several days of scouring Red Cross shelters, he found his two boys along with their mother in Medford. He thanked God for his good fortune. Even his ex seemed more receptive to him. Floods work in strange ways, he thought, and now the family would do its best to move in a positive direction. It would take a year, though, for Dave to recover from his bouts with stress and depression and to reorganize his life.

He took one last trip to the great river. After reaching the bank on the Oregon side, he looked at the river's calm, its serenity, and thought about how it had changed his life. This was his final look, as he would be moving away. Slowly he turned to walk back toward his car, but as an afterthought he turned around to get one last look at the Columbia. At that moment, several yards away from the shore, he caught sight of a large salmon jumping out of the water. Several seconds later, he saw another and another. He smiled to himself quietly, walking away and thinking that even the Columbia had been reborn.

About the Author

DAN AND HIS FIANCÉE, BONNIE, reside in Ellensburg, Washington. Dan was born in Tacoma and spent his early years growing up in Ellensburg. In his late teens and early twenties, he attended Central Washington State, pursuing an art degree, but other plans prevailed, and he left without a degree. He continued through his twenties working at odd jobs, including a miscellany of construction, agriculture, and forestry work and at one point as a laborer near Grand Coulee Dam in late 1970. He grew a familiarity with the Columbia Basin while working at positions in that area and over time recognized the significance of the Columbia River on the region's commerce.

In the 1980s he met his now ex-wife, who was from Pennsylvania, and the union brought them two children, Zanaya and Zachary. After a recession that affected a job that he held as a millwright in a log home manufacturer in 1981, it was time for a change. Dan obtained his nursing degree from a local junior college, and in 1986, the family moved to Pennsylvania, where Dan received his R.N. The author worked in various hospitals in and around the Philadelphia area in his twenty-six years of living there but gained his most valuable experiences as a clinical psychiatric nurse at a psychiatric facility where he worked for almost twenty years.

After spending twenty-six years on the East Coast and seeing that his children had become successful in their own rights, Dan looked to returning to the West. The dream became a reality, and in June of 2012, Dan and Bonnie headed west to Washington State and now reside in Ellensburg. The author now spends time with painting and is currently working on a second novel.

CPSIA information can be obtained at www.ICGtesting.com
Printed in the USA
BVOW02s1336160914

367049BV00001B/9/P